W9-CLF-487

THE HOPE CHEST

THE HOPE CHEST

KAREN SCHWABACH

RANDOM HOUSE NEW YORK

J Schwabach

This is a work of fiction. All incidents and dialogue, and all characters with the exception of some well-known historical and public figures, are products of the author's imagination and are not to be construed as real. Where real-life historical or public figures appear, the situations, incidents, and dialogues concerning those persons are fictional and are not intended to depict actual events or to change the fictional nature of the work. In all other respects, any resemblance to persons living or dead is entirely coincidental.

Photographs: Library of Congress, Prints & Photographs Division [LC-USZ62-119710], p. 263; Library of Congress, Prints & Photographs Division [LC-USZ62-79502], p. 265; Library of Congress, Prints & Photographs Division [LC-USZ62-126995], p. 266; Library of Congress, Prints & Photographs Division [LC-USZ62-19918], p. 267; Library of Congress, Prints & Photographs Division [LC-U9-10364-37], p. 268; Library of Congress, Prints & Photographs Division [LC-USZ62-75334], p. 271.

Published in the United States by Random House Children's Books,
a division of Random House, Inc., New York.

Visit us on the Web! www.randomhouse.com/kids

Educators and librarians, for a variety of teaching tools, visit us at
www.randomhouse.com/teachers

Library of Congress Cataloging-in-Publication Data
Schwabach, Karen
The Hope Chest / Karen Schwabach. — 1st ed.
p. cm.
Summary: When eleven-year-old Violet runs away from home in 1920 and takes the train to New York City to find her older sister who is a suffragist, she falls in with people her parents would call "the wrong sort," and ends up in Nashville, Tennessee, where "Suffs" and "Antis" are gathered, awaiting the crucial vote on the nineteenth amendment.
ISBN 978-0-375-84095-1 (trade) — ISBN 978-0-375-94095-8 (lib. bdg.)
1. Women—Suffrage—Juvenile fiction. [1. United States—History—1913–1921—Juvenile fiction. 2. Women—Suffrage—Fiction. 3. United States—History—1913–1921—Fiction. 4. Sisters—Fiction. 5. Women's rights—Fiction. 6. Tennessee—History—20th century—Fiction.]
I. Title.
PZ7.S3988Ho 2008 [Fic]—dc22 2006036692

Printed in the United States of America 10 9 8 7 6 5 4 3 2 1
First Edition

To Lisa Findlay
her story
and
to Veronica and Jessica Schwabach
may their votes always count

Contents

THE HOPE CHEST

1

The Stolen Letters

"GIVE THOSE TO ME AT ONCE, YOUNG LADY!"

Violet dropped the bundle of letters and looked up at her mother's angry face. She felt guilty, but only for a second. "They're mine," she said. "They're my letters, from my sister—they're addressed to *me*!"

Mother made a grab for the bundle and the two of them struggled, each gripping the letters with one fist. Mother used her other hand to try to pull Violet away from the desk by her pigtails, and Violet used her other hand to wrench her pigtails free. It was very unladylike—not at all graceful.

"How dare you?" Mother cried. "Going through my desk drawers—Violet Mayhew, I thought I brought you up better than that!"

"You hid them!" Violet screamed, managing to jerk

her hair and a few of the letters free. She lurched against Mother's desk, knocking over a vase of asters and a dreadful old hair wreath in a wooden frame. She retreated to the bedroom doorway. "I bet Chloe's been writing me for the whole time since you threw her out, and you let me think she'd forgotten all about me!"

"Violet, you know perfectly well your father and I always do what's best for you." Mother had decided to be calm and firm, but there were tears in the corners of her eyes.

Violet didn't care. She was too mad to care. "You hid Chloe's letters from me for three whole years. You *stole* them from me!"

Violet retreated out the door. Heavy footsteps thudded up the stairs behind her. Violet turned around and saw Father. It was his newspaper-reading time, and Violet and Mother had disturbed it.

"What in the name of Sam Hill is going on here?" Father demanded.

"I'm sorry, Arthur," said Mother. "Violet has stolen some letters from my desk drawer."

Violet backed up against the hall mirror. Father towered. He was broad and massive, like the bank where he worked. He had left his jacket downstairs, but he still looked imposing in a black broadcloth vest and trousers and a spotless white shirt with a high starched collar. He glared down at Violet through his gold-rimmed spectacles.

"Why aren't you downstairs reading to your brother?" he demanded.

Violet had no good answer. She had sat with Stephen but hadn't bothered to read to him since she'd finished all her Oz books. Instead, she'd written a letter to her cousin and had been looking through Mother's desk for a stamp when she found the letters.

"Give those back to your mother at once, young lady," said Father.

"They're addressed to me," Violet said. "From Chloe." She shifted toward the hall corner, toward the dog's-leg turn that led to the back stairway. Standing up to Father was a lot scarier than standing up to Mother, partly because he so seldom spoke to her. "I won't," she said.

"Then give them to me." Father held out his hand. "At once, young lady, or you are going to be in so much trouble it will make your head swim."

"I don't care," said Violet. She didn't. She was madder than she'd ever been in her life. They told her to be seen and not heard and to speak only when spoken to. They sent her sister away and stuck her with a brother who wouldn't even talk. Then they hid her own letters from her and called it *stealing* when she found them. It was wretched that just because a person happened to be eleven years old, that person didn't have any say in things at all—not even about getting to read her own letters.

Father moved toward Violet, a huge, threatening

tower of authority. Mother seemed to disappear from Violet's field of vision. Father always had a way of making Mother disappear.

Violet darted around the corner and clattered down the curving back staircase and out through the kitchen, where Eleanor, the cook, was making boiled custard. She slammed the screen door and ran all the way to the banks of the Susquehanna River.

She had only grabbed a few letters, from the middle of the stack. The postmark on the first envelope was from 1918, two years ago. She sat down at her favorite spot, under an old elm tree that grew on the riverbank, and began to read.

New York City
Saturday, November 9, 1918

Dear Violet,

Well, I voted! It was nothing like Father warned me. There were no gangs of hoodlums standing at the top of the steps to throw down voters from the opposition party. I did not lose my femininity. I didn't have to drag my skirts through the mud and muck of national politics — my skirts are eight inches from the ground, and the muck of national politics turned out not to be that deep this year. There were thousands of women voting, and yet New York did not have a Bolshevist revolution. (Not yet, anyway. It's only been a few days.)

Did the false armistice happen in Susquehanna too? Thursday the newsboys were out on the streets hollering that the War was over. I was treating influenza patients on the fifth floor of a tenement house, and everybody dashed down the stairs and out into the street, cheering and throwing their hats in the air. But then it turned out not to be true, of course.

Everyone says the War can't last much longer now. A lot of the countries in Europe have given women the vote now, you know. Some of them have only given it to women whose sons were killed in the War. That makes me really angry — as if women are only as good as men if their sons die. But the United States doesn't even have that.

At least women can vote in New York State now. That makes sixteen states, plus the territory of Alaska. Ah, Alaska! Speaking of soldiers, how is Stephen doing? I hope you aren't reading the war news to him. I know Father always says that that's what he'll want to hear, but somehow that doesn't seem very likely to me.

Write if you can. The address is on the envelope.

Your loving sister,

Chloe

Violet smiled because the letter sounded so much like Chloe. And Alaska—Chloe had always wanted to go to Alaska. She'd taken out every book the library had about Alaska, and she'd drawn Violet a picture of an Eskimo driving a dogsled. Violet had asked for an igloo too, but Chloe had said that Alaskan Eskimos didn't live in igloos. Violet looked at the envelope. The address was somewhere in New York City—Henry Street.

The next letter gave her a jolt.

November 20, 1918

Dear Violet,

I can't tell you how sorry I am about Flossie. You know Father wouldn't let me in to see you, don't you? I drove up as soon as I heard about it from Cousin Helen and was in Susquehanna the next morning (had to stop in Scranton overnight after the Hope Chest blew a tire — its second on the trip — and it was too dark to see to change it). Mother wanted to let me in, I think, but Father said no, and all I could think of was you all alone upstairs in our old bedroom with your thoughts.

I wish I could call, but even if I had enough money for long distance, Father would just hang up. Write to me, all right? I want to know how you're doing. And wear your face mask every time you go out so you don't get the flu.

Love,

Chloe

Violet felt a sharp twist in her stomach. Reading the letter made it feel as if her best friend, Flossie, had just died yesterday instead of almost two years ago. It had happened right near where she was sitting now, on the banks of the Susquehanna—she and Flossie were playing Nellie Bly. Nellie Bly was a newspaper reporter who reported the War from the trenches on the western front, and Flossie wanted to grow up to be just like her. So that day they were playing that Flossie was Nellie Bly and Violet was a captured German soldier. Only suddenly Flossie had complained of a backache, and then she had gotten a nosebleed, and Violet had said, "Your ear's bleeding, Flossie." And by the time she'd helped Flossie home, Flossie was bleeding out of both ears and her nose and couldn't talk.

That was the influenza—like getting run over by a steam train. Not just sniffles, but blood pouring out of your nose and ears. People didn't understand how the disease could hit that hard, could kill so many people, when it was only the flu. Except that after 1918, it would never be "only the flu" again.

Violet clenched the letter in her hand and was furious

at Mother and Father. In those awful bleak days after Flossie died, it would have meant a lot to have Chloe sitting at the foot of her bed again, talking to her and telling her stories. She couldn't believe Mother and Father had sent Chloe away when Violet needed her, just because Chloe was a New Woman who wanted to vote and have a job of her own. She was still Chloe.

Violet read the next letter.

December 1, 1918

Dear Violet,

How are you?

The influenza is really bad here. I treated eighty-five patients in the tenements behind Hester Street yesterday. I start at the bottom of one building and work my way up, calling on patients, and then when I get to the roof, I step across onto the next building and work my way down. Don't worry, there's no space in between the buildings! I called on one family where the mother, father, and six children were all sick in one little room and all huddled into one bed. None of them spoke any English.

So far I haven't gotten the flu (touch wood) because I'm careful to wear my mask all the time. Are you wearing yours? They also gave all of us public health nurses an inoculation at the Henry Street Settlement

House, but we think that it's a placebo — a fake shot, to make us think we're protected.

The other night I had a funny accident. I was coming home in the dark after seeing 107 patients, and I crashed right into a young man carrying a shovel. We both went sprawling into the gutter, which was not exactly clean. . . . I guess there are still more horses than motorcars in New York! It turned out the poor fellow had been digging graves, which is a pretty big job these days. . . . Anyway, he was very polite and forgiving and walked me home.

Please write and let me know how you're doing. I think about you all the time.

Love,

Chloe

That letter started stupid tears in Violet's eyes again, and she dashed them away with the sleeve of her middy blouse. She thought about Chloe all the time too. So that was what Chloe was doing—being a public health nurse. During the huge scene after Chloe bought the Hope Chest, Chloe had shouted something about wanting to do something *meaningful* with her life. Mother had cried and asked her what wasn't meaningful about marrying an up-and-coming man like Mr. Russell (or was it Mr. Rice?) and having beautiful babies?

Violet, listening on the stairs, had known just what

Chloe meant. At school Violet's class was knitting squares to make blankets for French war orphans. Miss Smedley read to the class—*Ivanhoe* was what she was reading to them just then—for half an hour each day while they knitted. And although Miss Smedley tried to make a game of it by keeping score of who knitted more squares—the boys or the girls—to Violet, knitting those squares seemed like the most important thing she had ever done in her life. She felt as though she was part of something huge, something vital, something that involved the whole world. Or at least much more of the world than she had ever seen.

Mr. Rice (or was it Mr. Russell?) had no very high opinion of women working, or voting, or doing anything interesting. Both Mr. R.'s worked for Father at the bank, and they still came to Sunday dinner every week, even though Chloe was no longer around for either of them to marry. Last Sunday they'd tried to outdo each other making jokes about women voting.

"Can you imagine if women were actually allowed to vote?" Mr. Russell had asked. "Elections would have to go on for days, with all those women standing in the voting booths, not being able to make up their minds."

"Not only that, but they'd be standing up on their little tippy toes, trying to peer into the other booths to see who the other women were voting for," said Mr. Rice.

Violet couldn't imagine why Mother and Father had

thought Chloe would marry either one of them. She eagerly unfolded the next letter.

December 20, 1918

Dear Violet,

Merry Christmas! I've been thinking about you a lot. I wish I could come see you for Christmas, but Father would just slam the door in my face again — so it would be a waste of gasoline, at more than twenty cents a gallon. (Did I tell you the Hope Chest gets twenty-five miles to the gallon, though? It's great!) The influenza seems to be spreading a little less this week — touch wood. I hope you are still well. A friend of mine was very bad with it, but he's better now, and I think he will live. It was scary, though.

The federal government has started deporting foreign-born radicals to Russia. Can you imagine? A lot of them didn't even come from Russia. Some of them have lived in this country nearly all their lives. But I guess that's what happens when you have a war. People start hating immigrants. I think there are people who just need someone to hate. I just hope they don't deport all of them. Some of them are such dear people.

I hope you can come to New York City one day. You

never saw a place so alive, with so many different ideas being talked about in so many different languages. New York City is a college education in itself. Still, I hope that you, at least, will find a way to go to college, and I mean a whole four years of it.

Love,

Chloe

Violet put the letter down and looked out at the muddy waters of the Susquehanna slipping by. Chloe made what their mother had always called "the wrong sort of people" sound really interesting, which Violet had always suspected they might be. She made them sound downright uplifting. Wasn't it just like their parents to want to keep Violet away from anything interesting! Chloe was wrong about Violet finding a way to go to college, though. Violet didn't want to go to college—school was boring, and the sooner she was out of it the better. Besides, Father was against college for girls.

The next thing in the pile wasn't a letter but a slender tin-framed snapshot. Stephen and Chloe, when they were teenagers, sat stiffly in their Sunday best and held Violet, who wore a white dress with enormous skirts that covered both their laps. She had been a plain baby, Violet thought, just like she was a plain girl—with straight brown hair that had never curled and never would and a snub nose and ordinary brown eyes. Mother must have stuck the picture into the pile of letters, but why? So that she would remember what Chloe looked like? Or was she trying to hide Chloe so she could forget her?

January 15, 1919

Dear Violet,

Happy New Year! I would have written sooner, but there have been some bad relapses in flu cases, as well as some other things that have been keeping me very busy. I hope you are thinking about what I said about college — I know it seems far away when you are in fourth grade. College arms you to fight the great battles. I learned that from Miss Lillian Wald; she's the founder of the Henry Street Settlement House, where I'm doing my nurse training. She invented public health nursing, you know. She says the influenza has been a baptism by fire for all of her trainees. I hope I never see anything worse.

Speaking of battles, it looks as though Congress is going to take up the Susan B. Anthony Amendment when it reconvenes. That's the amendment poor Miss Anthony wrote back in 1878. Congress voted it down back then — to think women could have gotten the vote forty years ago! It needs a two-thirds vote of both houses of Congress to pass, which means it's going to be a huge knock-down, drag-out fight. And Congress has defeated it before. If they do pass it, it will go to the states for ratification. And then it will be part of our U.S. Constitution.

Part of me really wants to go to Washington to help Miss Alice Paul and the National Woman's Party work for that amendment. But I also want to stay here and finish my nurse's training. (Especially now that my baptism by fire is over — touch wood and cross fingers!) There are other things that make me want to stay in New York too. But a woman shouldn't let herself be ruled by those sorts of things.

Love,
Chloe

Violet couldn't figure out what the last two sentences of that letter meant. Chloe's life in New York sounded thrilling. Violet imagined Chloe climbing up and down towering tenement buildings, risking death (by influenza or falling off a roof) to bring help and hope to hundreds of suffering people. It sounded a lot more exciting than marrying one of the Mr. R.'s. Violet eagerly opened the next letter.

February 18, 1919

Dear Violet,

You still haven't written back to me. I hope you're not still angry with me for leaving. You know I really couldn't do anything else. I didn't want to marry Mr. Russell (or whoever else they found for me!) and turn into a good little helpmeet, hosting dinner parties and having babies and never again having a thought or idea or dream of my own.

I wonder if Mother ever had a dream before she married Father? Well, it's too late for me to ask her now. Last week I drove the Hope Chest out to Long Island with some girls from one of the worst tenements on Hester Street. None of them had ever seen an open field before. They couldn't believe all the space. I wish you could have been with us. The Hope Chest got two flat tires, one on the way there and one on the way back, but fortunately a friend of mine showed me how to patch them myself. Everyone agrees that a lady motorist should know how to change a tire, but considering how often they burst, I'm glad I know how to patch them now as well.

Some people think that us suffragists (or is it we suffragists?) hate men, but that's not true at all. Lots of men are really nice, like my friend who showed me how to patch tires. There's a difference between liking men and wanting to have them run your whole life.

Well, that's neither here nor there. I hope you are getting along all right. I remember that when I was in *eighth grade and my friend Dottie Armitage died of consumption, I didn't want to be friends with anyone else for a long time. I thought that would be somehow disloyal to Dottie. It wasn't true, though, and I hope you know it isn't true about Flossie either. When a friend dies, some of her always stays inside of us. Write back if you can.*

Love,
Chloe

Violet felt peculiar—it was as if Chloe had read her mind. Back then, that is. She had felt just that way, when her grief started to ease enough that she could sometimes laugh and have fun and want to be with people again. She'd felt as if she'd be betraying Flossie if she made other friends. Violet threw the letter angrily down on the riverbank beside her. It would have been great to read this letter back then.

The last letter was just a note.

April 15, 1919

Dear Violet,

This clipping is a poem that was in the newspaper the other day. It's called "Aftermath," and it's by a man named Siegfried Sassoon, who was in the British army. I wish you'd read it to Stephen.

You know there's going to be a League of Nations — everyone says we will never have a war again. I hope that's true.

Violet looked in the envelope, but there was no clipping. Either it had fallen out or Mother had taken it when she'd read the letter.

That was what made Violet snap. Mother had read all these letters. Maybe Father too, but it was Mother who she felt ought to have known better. Mother had kept Chloe's interesting news and comforting thoughts from Violet when Violet had needed them most. And there were more letters, besides these few that Violet had managed to rescue. Violet knew they wouldn't be in the desk anymore. They'd be hidden somewhere she couldn't find them. Or even burned.

All her life, Violet had accepted that her parents made decisions, and whether Violet liked it or not, that was the way things were. But this was too much. The letters had been written just for her, by Chloe, the only person in the family who had ever told her anything except how to behave. And she hadn't stolen them; they'd been stolen from her. It was completely unfair, and Violet wasn't going to put up with it.

2

The Dying Mrs. Renwick

VIOLET WISHED SHE HAD MORE COMFORTABLE clothes to run away in.

Her navy blue pleated skirt and matching sailor's middy blouse were what Mother called a compromise. Mother liked to dress Violet in fluffy white dresses with lots of petticoats, a sash and ribbons of violet satin, and a hat with artificial violets around the brim. Violet would have preferred overalls. She had seen girls' overalls advertised in the Sears, Roebuck catalog, although she'd never seen anyone actually wearing them. They looked very convenient and serviceable. Violet had ruined several white dresses while exploring along the muddy banks of the Susquehanna River and lost two hats with violets around the brim. Then Mother had given up on the white dresses with violet trim. As far as Violet was concerned, her navy blue clothes weren't a compromise at all. Violet wanted overalls.

When Violet had finally gone home, after an hour or two of squatting among the trees on the bank watching the Susquehanna water slide indifferently past, she'd been sent to her room without dinner. Violet had tucked the letters into her bloomers, just above the band of elastic around her knee, and pulled her stockings up over them and buttoned the garters to her undervest before she got home. When Mother asked her for the letters, Violet told her she'd thrown them in the river.

Now it was morning, and Violet sat on an itchy mohair-covered train seat and stared out the train window at the smokestacks and the soot-blackened brick buildings chugging by. She was on her way to New York City. She was through with Mother and Father and their rules. She was going to the Henry Street Settlement House, and she was going to find Chloe.

Before she left, Chloe had told Violet about settlement houses—they were mostly started in bad neighborhoods in the big cities by young college men and women. They lived in the settlement houses and did whatever they could to help out—taught English classes, took care of sick people, organized children's clubs. There were even some workers in the settlement houses who called themselves social workers, although Violet wasn't quite sure what those were. It had something to do with socialism.

Socialism, Chloe had once explained to her, meant the idea that people should take care of each other instead of just themselves.

Well, Violet was big enough to take care of herself and whoever else needed it. She had snuck out of the house in the very first morning light, taking her savings of $3.92 tied up in a handkerchief pinned inside her middy blouse. Violet couldn't face another scene—she hated scenes—and besides, she very much doubted that she would have been able to leave if there had been a fight, since unlike Chloe, she was only eleven and didn't have the Hope Chest.

She remembered the final scene when Chloe had left and never come back. Father and Chloe had yelled at each other at the door. Mostly Father. Mother had stood behind him saying, "Arthur, the neighbors!" Violet had sat at the top of the stairs, out of everyone's sight. She had hugged her knees to her chest, bunched up into a tight little ball of terror as Father's bellowing rang through the hall and made the crystal in the chandelier hum. Stephen had been in the front parlor, presumably studying the wallpaper. Violet had heard the front door slam shut and the creaking of the crank that started the Hope Chest, then the sudden roar of the Hope Chest's engine as Chloe drove away.

The Hope Chest had been the final straw, as far as Father was concerned. Not the votes for women nonsense, not the damn-fool crazy college ideas, not Chloe's insisting that she wanted to do something meaningful, but the Hope Chest.

Granny Mayhew was Father's mother. When she died in 1914, she had left $250 each to Violet and Chloe for their hope chests and $500 to Stephen for his education.

A hope chest was a big wooden trunk that a girl was supposed to fill with things she'd need when she was married—tablecloths and bed linens and dishes and things like that. But of course money could be a lot more useful than tablecloths. Violet tried not to think about what she would have done with that $250 if they ever really let her have it—travel, maybe to South America. They never would, of course. Not after what Chloe had done with her hope chest money. No, they'd keep it from Violet—keep it safe for her, as Mother would say—and make her spend it to set up housekeeping with some husband. Two hundred and fifty dollars' worth of furniture and linens and housekeeping stuff. The thought of it was oppressive, like high walls closing in on her. But there was nothing she could do about it.

Stephen had taken his $500 and enrolled at Cornell University. A year later he had gone off to Canada—way back in 1915, long before America entered the War. He had enlisted in the Canadian army and been sent to France to fight the Germans. A few Americans did that. You heard a lot in those days about martyred Belgium, and it made some people mad that America wasn't getting into the War. By the time American boys were being conscripted into the army and sent overseas in late 1917, Stephen was already back—or what was left of him.

Chloe had somehow convinced Father to let her go to college. Not a big university like Cornell, of course, but a junior college. Violet wasn't sure how this had been accomplished. Chloe had always been able to talk to Father more than Violet had, at least back when they were still speaking to each other. At the time, Violet was mainly concerned that Chloe was going away—although not very far—and wasn't going to sit at the foot of her bed and tell her stories every night or draw her pictures of Alaska. But then college had led to talk about the settlement houses and being a nurse. And then Chloe had taken her hope chest money, all of it, and bought a used Model T Ford. She even had the effrontery to name it the Hope Chest.

So it was for sure that Violet wasn't ever going to get $250. She'd had $3.92 in a jar under her bed, saved up from birthdays and her allowance. It was a remarkable sum, or so she'd always thought, until she bought the train ticket to New York. It had cost $3.25. She'd tried to buy a half-price ticket, claiming she was under eight, but the ticket clerk had told her in a bored voice that she could either be old enough to travel to New York City by herself or young enough to travel at half fare, but not both. And Violet didn't dare argue, since she was nervous about the trip to New York, and besides, she really wasn't under eight.

Well, Chloe would be glad that Violet was coming to live with her. Violet could go to school in New York, and

Mother could devote all her time to Stephen. And Father would be positively glad Violet was gone. Mother might worry what the neighbors would think, but Father probably wouldn't even care about that. They'd both be glad. They'd gotten rid of Chloe, and now . . .

Violet felt a tear trickle itchily down the side of her nose, and she wiped it away with her sleeve.

"Tickets!" The conductor was coming through the car. Violet nervously held out her ticket, trying to look like she rode on trains all the time.

The conductor read the ticket and frowned at her. "Kind of young to be going to New York City alone, aren't you, miss?"

"I'm almost twelve," said Violet defensively.

The conductor shrugged, punched a hole in the ticket, and handed it back to her.

At the next stop a woman got on and took the seat across from Violet. Violet could tell at once that she was a meddlesome woman. She was dressed in the fashion of twenty years ago, in a sweeping black bombazine gown, and she smelled of mothballs. She was tightly corseted into a perfect S shape, with a pigeon bosom, a wasp waist, and a bustle to exaggerate her rear end. On her head she wore a black hat with an enormous lopsided brim—two feet to starboard and a foot and a half to port, Father would have said. The corpse of a large bird, dyed a dismal purple, was diving into a mass of black ribbons heaped around the crown of the hat.

Involuntarily Violet clutched at her own neat straw hat, as if the woman might try to trade with her.

The woman sat down stiffly and with great difficulty. She tilted her head back slightly, probably to balance her hat, and scowled down her nose at Violet.

"*I,*" she said with great emphasis, "am Mrs. Albert Renwick of Huntington, Long Island."

"Pleased to meet you," Violet lied. Mother would probably have wanted Violet to stand up and curtsy.

"And you?" said Mrs. Renwick.

"Miss Violet Mayhew of Susquehanna, Pennsylvania," Violet said.

Mrs. Renwick twitched her nose suspiciously, as if she thought Violet might be making fun of her. "You're very small to be traveling alone. Where are you going?"

"New York City," said Violet, thinking it was none of Mrs. Renwick's business.

"And what takes you there, if I may ask?"

"I'm going to visit my sister. My grown-up sister."

"Young ladies," said Mrs. Renwick, "should not travel unaccompanied on the train. Is your sister married?"

"No," said Violet shortly.

"Then why is she not living with your parents? Are your parents still living?"

"Yes," said Violet. "But they're very busy with my brother, Stephen. He's still recovering from the War." Violet hoped that would silence Mrs. Renwick. A recovering war veteran was a very impressive thing to have in the family.

"All the more reason your sister ought to have stayed home to help. In my day a girl's greatest joy was being of service to her brothers. I myself worked my fingers to the bone in a glove factory to pay my brother's tuition at Harvard. And I felt privileged to do so," Mrs. Renwick said defiantly, as if Violet had suggested she hadn't. "Privileged to do so. But I suppose your sister is one of these New Women." She made it sound like a disease.

Violet glanced around surreptitiously for another empty seat. It would be very rude to get up and walk away from Mrs. Renwick, but Mrs. Renwick was pretty rude herself.

Mrs. Renwick seemed to sense what was on Violet's mind and changed the subject. "I am dying, you know, Violet," she said.

Violet stared at her. She felt bad for thinking uncharitable thoughts of Mrs. Renwick. "I'm sorry."

"Too kind," Mrs. Renwick murmured.

"What of?" said Violet, and then realized that this was an extremely rude question.

Mrs. Renwick didn't seem to think so. "Have you heard of tuberculosis?"

"Yes," said Violet. Regretting she'd been rude, she added, "I'm sorry you have tuberculosis, Mrs. Renwick."

"I do not have tuberculosis," said Mrs. Renwick.

Violet stared again. "But I thought you said . . ."

"Those foolish doctors don't know what I have," said Mrs. Renwick with proud finality.

"Oh," said Violet.

"Dozens of doctors have seen me, and none of them can say what is the matter with me. Not one."

"Maybe nothing's the matter with you," Violet ventured.

"Excuse me. Are *you* a doctor?" asked Mrs. Renwick coldly.

"Of course not," said Violet, irritated.

"I should think not," said Mrs. Renwick. "It's a revolting thing for a female to do, becoming a doctor. Absolutely revolting."

Since this was what Father had always said and Mother had (as always) agreed with him, Violet figured that was what most people thought. She had never wanted to be a doctor herself. She'd never really thought about being anything. She had known what was in her future—the hope chest, and the marriage, and that was it.

But Chloe had wanted to be a nurse. And Flossie, before she died in the Influenza, had wanted to be a reporter. And some of Flossie would always be in her—Violet remembered that from Chloe's letter.

That was why Violet found herself answering, "I don't want to be a doctor. I want to be a reporter."

Mrs. Renwick gaped. "A re-*what*-er?"

"A reporter," said Violet. "Like Nellie Bly. She filed news from the trenches in Europe, you know. During the War." Somehow Violet felt that she had to say this to Mrs. Renwick for Flossie's sake.

"How absolutely appalling," said Mrs. Renwick,

rolling her eyes upward and fluttering her eyelashes at the same time, which had the disconcerting effect of making her eyes go all white. "A female, in the trenches!"

"There were plenty of females in the trenches," Violet said. "At the end, the Germans were sending in women, and boys fourteen years old. And the Russians—"

"A young lady does not need to know anything about trenches," Mrs. Renwick interrupted firmly. "Nor about Germans and Russians. Let us change the subject. Where does your sister live?"

Violet felt instantly dejected. She didn't know where Chloe lived. The return address on the envelopes was 265 Henry Street, New York City, but she had no idea where that was. She had a vague idea that New York was bigger than Susquehanna, Pennsylvania. This part of her plan was not figured out too well.

Mrs. Renwick was watching her closely. "I'm not sure exactly where," said Violet.

"Ah. Well, she's meeting you at the station, anyway," Mrs. Renwick said. And having settled Violet's travel arrangements to her satisfaction, she went back to the main problem. "Violet, a female can't be a reporter, and that's final."

Violet didn't know what to say. She knew it was very wrong to contradict adults. And she didn't even really want to be a reporter. That had been Flossie's dream. Chloe had always told her that a girl could be anything she wanted to be. So had Violet's sixth-grade teacher,

Miss Elliott. But Violet had certainly never heard that from anyone else.

So she bit back any response. She turned and looked out the window at a smoke-blackened brick factory, its hundreds of windowpanes too grimy to see through.

"I'm glad you've decided to see reason," said Mrs. Renwick. "I'm an old woman, and a dying woman to boot, and my words are worth hearing. A woman can't be anything she wants to be, because that's not the way the good Lord made us. He made us to be the helpmeets of men and to be protected by them. If women go out being doctors and reporters and demanding to vote, then how can they expect men to protect them anymore?"

Violet hadn't said anything about voting. Getting the right to vote was Chloe's project. Father had said that it was sending Chloe off to college that had filled her head with damn-fool crazy ideas, but Violet knew that Chloe's head had been filled with crazy ideas before. Violet didn't much care about voting. She was only eleven, and nobody was talking about giving eleven-year-olds the vote.

Mrs. Renwick went on, "The Lord has given females the wonderful gift of being able to bear children, and that's the work that women do. So let's hear no more of this nonsense about wanting to be a reporter. Now, how many children do you want to have, Violet?"

Violet felt deflated. She flopped back on the prickly green train seat, even though she could hear Mother in her head scolding that a lady doesn't ever let her back touch the back of her chair. There was no point in arguing with Mrs. Renwick, even less point than there had ever been in arguing with Mother or Father. What Mrs. Renwick was saying was the same thing that Violet had heard again and again for as long as she could remember.

"Seven," Violet said. People were always asking her how many children she wanted, just as they asked boys what they wanted to be when they grew up. She had learned that seven was a very impressive answer.

Certainly it impressed Mrs. Renwick. "Seven! Gracious, that's quite a lot, my dear!"

Violet managed a smile. Mother had always told her, "Smile even if it breaks your face."

"Well, that's a much better idea than being a reporter. Seven! My, aren't you an ambitious little chick." Mrs. Renwick leaned forward creakily to pinch Violet's cheek, which Violet submitted to despite an overwhelming smell of mothballs.

"Here!" Mrs. Renwick waved to the candy butcher, who was coming down the aisle with his box-shaped tray strapped to his belly. "A Tootsie Roll for the young lady, please. No, make it two Tootsie Rolls."

The man gave Violet the candy and accepted a nickel from Mrs. Renwick. "Anything for yourself, ma'am?"

"Oh no, not for me." Mrs. Renwick's enthusiasm waned suddenly and she did the thing with her eyelids again. Violet looked hastily away. "I'm not well, you know. . . . Dying, in fact. . . ."

But the candy butcher hadn't listened past "no" and was off down the aisle again calling, "Candy!"

Violet bit into a Tootsie Roll and let the burned-chocolate taste run over her tongue. She looked at the dying Mrs. Renwick (whom she had politely thanked, of course) and thought that if growing up meant having seven children and wearing a dead bird on her head, Violet would rather have been born a boy.

3

Meeting Myrtle

THE TRAIN WAS STUCK FOR A LONG TIME IN Scranton because of some sort of trouble on the tracks. It was evening when it pulled into New York.

The station was huge. Violet bid a hasty farewell to Mrs. Renwick and sped away, trying to look like she knew where she was going. She was conscious that other people had suitcases and even trunks, which colored men in dark uniforms and red caps wheeled along for them on carts. She had nothing at all but her letters from Chloe and sixty-seven cents pinned in a handkerchief inside her blouse. The train station went on and on, its stone floors and high, vaulted ceilings echoing with the voices of hundreds of people.

Now what? It was hard to think straight with all this noise. New York was somehow much louder than Violet had imagined. Violet looked over her shoulder to see if Mrs. Renwick was still watching her, but Mrs. Renwick was gone. Violet was glad but also scared. She needed to ask directions, and she did not know how. A policeman in a blue uniform stood beside an iron pillar, swinging his stick. Speaking to adults was a dangerous business. One wrong word could get you sent to your room without dinner.

How did you address a police officer? Girls weren't supposed to say "sir"—that was for boys and the Wrong Sort of People. You should call men "Mr." something, but she didn't know the police officer's name. And speaking without being spoken to was always wrong.

Violet took a deep breath. If she didn't break any of these rules, she was going to be stuck in this train station forever.

"Excuse me, sir, can you tell me the way out of the train station?"

The policeman leaned down and peered at her as if she were very small. "The exit's at the top of the stairs, little girl. Where's your mama?"

"She's . . . my sister's waiting for me," Violet said hastily.

"Uh-huh." The policeman looked suspicious. "Well, why don't you just stand right here with me, and we'll wait for your sister together."

Violet couldn't think what to do. If she ran away, the policeman might chase after her. She stood beside him, thinking fast—how was she going to get away so she could find Henry Street and Chloe?

"What does your sister look like?" the policeman asked.

"She's tall and . . . Oh, there she is!" Violet took off running, calling over her shoulder, "Thank you, sir!"

Violet hadn't seen Chloe, of course. But it fooled the policeman. She ran up the stone staircase and squeezed into the brass-and-glass revolving door next to a young woman in a green hat topped with a tall upright ruffle of starched silk like a crown. She smiled up at the woman adoringly in case the policeman was still watching her.

With a thumping swish, the revolving door dumped Violet out onto the sidewalk. It was much darker out than she'd expected. It was evening of a long August day, but the street was a canyon between high granite and cast-iron skyscrapers, and the sun didn't reach the bottom. Motorcars, streetcars, and horse-drawn wagons rumbled by, guided by electric or kerosene lamps mounted on the front. People pushed past Violet, and she stumbled back against the granite wall of the train station. New York was loud, and fast, and scary, and she didn't like it.

"Hey!" A boy in knee britches pushed her. "This is my section. Shove off." He picked up an armload of newspapers and threw himself into the crowd, shouting, "Extra! Extra! Red Army advances on Warsaw; Poland sues for peace!"

The crowd tossed the boy around like a kernel of

popcorn in a shaking pan until he popped back out. He bumped up against the wall and shook his fist at Violet. "I said get lost. Go find your own sidewalk."

He shoved Violet again, and she stumbled out into the moving crowd.

Terrified, Violet struggled to stay upright. The crowd caught her and carried her along. She didn't know where she was going. She wanted to ask if anybody knew the way to Henry Street, but nobody even looked at her. Once she was knocked off the sidewalk into the street, and there was a squeal of brakes and the blast of a long, curled brass car horn. Violet scrambled hastily up onto the sidewalk and tried to stay closer to the walls. She felt like Dorothy caught up in the cyclone or Alice falling down the rabbit hole.

Sometimes the crowd crossed streets—she could tell because the sidewalks beneath her feet turned to asphalt road and then back into sidewalk again. Violet could see nothing but the shoulders of men's coats and women's dresses and here and there the face of someone her own age. Unlike her, they seemed able to weave expertly through the people, going whichever way they wanted.

After what seemed like hours, Violet found herself free of the crowd. It was dark now, or almost dark—it was hard to tell, because the massive iron bulk of the elevated railway covered the sidewalk and part of the street like a roof, and electric signs over shop windows turned everything an eerie orange. New York was huger than Violet had imagined, and she had no idea how she was going to find Chloe. She was beginning to wish she had never left Susquehanna.

The sounds of ragtime music jingled from some of the shops, and men in loose-fitting suits and straw boater hats lounged around the doorways. From one shop with a sign out front that said *Barbizon Wigs Best Quality,* Violet heard a woman singing along with a nickelodeon tinnily playing a song that had been popular a few months ago:

How you gonna keep 'em down on the farm
After they've seen Paree?
How you gonna keep 'em from disappearing,
Jazzing around, and painting the town?
How you gonna keep 'em away from harm?
That's a mystery.

As Violet passed a group of men lounging in front of a candy store, one of them reached out and grabbed her arm. "Hey, baby, come on in and dance with me. Let's shake a leg!"

"Let go of me!" Violet kicked at his shins. She thought he smelled strongly of liquor, but that couldn't be. Alcohol had been illegal in the United States ever since the Volstead Act took effect in January.

The stupid man just laughed, but one of the others shoved him and said, "Cheese it, Stan. That ain't no broad; that's just a kid."

Stan let go. Frightened and disgusted, Violet hurried away. After that, she stayed well away from the doorways, skirting inside the El's giant iron legs. She kept walking, fast. She didn't know where she was going, but she didn't like where she was.

A train thundered overhead, making the iron frame of the El creak and the sidewalk under Violet's feet tremble. There was an enormous, crashing roar, as if the El were collapsing. Coal smoke filled her lungs and made her eyes smart. Violet stumbled blindly, unable to see but desperate to get out from under the crumbling Elevated.

Panicking, she stumbled into the street and slipped on something. She skidded, flailing her arms, trying to stay balanced. Then she hit the pavement with a smack that rattled her teeth. It took her a moment to catch her breath enough to smell what she'd slipped on. Horse dung.

A hand grabbed her arm. "Hey! Are you trying to get run over, or what?"

Violet was ready to give up on New York. She had a confused idea that the easiest way to do that was just to stay where she was. Getting up was painful. She climbed gingerly onto the curb. Someone was brushing vigorously at the back of her skirt. "Now your dress is all dirty!"

Violet turned to see who had pulled her out of the gutter.

It was a black girl—colored, Violet corrected herself. Nice people said colored. The girl only came up to Violet's shoulder, but she was dressed in a maid's uniform—a blue-and-white-striped old-fashioned dress that came almost to her ankles, a white apron that tied behind with a big bow, and a quaint white mobcap that looked like it belonged two centuries in the past. One small braid had worked its way free from the cap. A badge on her dress said *Girls' Training Institute.*

"Are you all right?" said the girl, who was still brushing Violet off.

"Yes, I'm all right. But the El just collapsed. Was anybody hurt?" Violet looked around fearfully, expecting to see wreckage and smoke.

The girl glanced over Violet's shoulder. "The El wasn't collapsing; it was just going by," she said, sounding amused. Violet turned and saw to her embarrassment the dark outline of the El track behind her, apparently intact.

"You must not be from around here," said the girl, looking at Violet critically. "Where are you trying to get to?"

"The Henry Street Settlement House," said Violet.

"Boy, are you lost," said the girl. "Come on." She took Violet's arm and led her down the street. "My name's Myrtle Davies. What's yours?"

Violet had never been introduced to a colored person before, let alone introduced herself. She decided to say the same thing she had to Mrs. Renwick. "I am Miss Violet Mayhew of Susquehanna, Pennsylvania."

"Susquehanna, Pennsylvania? No wonder you're

lost," said Myrtle. "I'm surprised they let you out on your own."

"You're out on your own," Violet pointed out, irritated. Myrtle looked a lot younger than Violet.

"But I know my way around," said Myrtle. "And I'm city-born. I grew up in Washington, D.C."

Grew up, Violet thought, was an exaggeration. The girl couldn't be older than eight. "What are you doing in New York, then?"

"I was sent here to attend the Girls' Training Institute." Myrtle said the last three words in a high, nasal singsong that communicated quite clearly that she loathed the place. "We cross here—stop!" Myrtle grabbed the square collar of Violet's blouse just as a steam-powered automobile zoomed down the street.

"What are they training you for?" Violet asked.

"Nothing," said Myrtle with a shrug, sidestepping a mound of horse manure. "I try not to spend too much time there, to tell the truth."

"Well, but is it a school?" said Violet, getting irritated again. "Or what?"

"It's supposed to be a school." Myrtle shrugged again. "It trains colored girls to be maids. They sent me here because the training institutes in D.C. won't take girls my age. I'm ten, and they said you have to be twelve."

"Who sent you?" said Violet, thinking that Myrtle barely looked eight, let alone ten. But she'd heard all her life that colored people were Different, so maybe they grew differently. "Your parents?"

"My parents are dead," said Myrtle. "The ladies at church sent me."

"Oh." It was getting dark. They turned into a narrow street with wagons parked all along both sides of it. Some were unhitched; the dark shapes of horses fidgeted and stamped between the shafts of others. Buildings loomed overhead, and most of the streetlights were broken. Violet suddenly felt cold, even though it was an August night. This whole street seemed foreign and dangerous and smelled overwhelmingly of horseradish. To distract herself, Violet said, "Don't you want to be a maid, then?"

"Would you?" said Myrtle.

"Of course not," said Violet. She had an odd feeling that Myrtle's situation was a little like her own—except that Violet had marriage looming in front of her and Myrtle had being a maid. But they were both caged in by other people's plans for them, with no hope of escape. Except that Violet *was* escaping.

"I'm sorry about your parents," Violet added belatedly. She thought about what it must be like to have both your parents dead. Father rarely spoke to her, and Mother was mostly in the business of handing out rules. They were never warm or friendly like parents she'd read about in books. Still, not having them would make the world a very strange place. Like a house without a roof.

"Thank you," said Myrtle with dignity.

A sharp pickles-and-onions smell cut through the

horseradish and manure, and Violet realized how hungry she was. She looked around for the source.

There! Violet saw a pushcart on two huge wooden wagon wheels topped by a big canvas umbrella. A kerosene lantern hanging from the umbrella pole shed just enough light for Violet to make out the words painted on the side: *Hot Dogs Lemonade.*

The warm light from the lantern made the street seem less scary. "Let's get a hot dog, Myrtle," Violet said.

"I don't have any money," Myrtle said.

"That's okay. I do." Violet turned to the hot dog seller, a man in a long white apron and plaid cloth cap. "Two hot . . . er, how much are they, please?"

"Five cents each," the man said. He had a foreign accent. "Five cents for lemonade—you gotta drink it here, though, 'cause I only got the one glass."

Violet looked at the smudged glass, which he held out for her inspection, and at the open bucket of lemonade hanging on the side of the cart. She was thirsty, but . . .

"Two hot dogs, please," she said. The man took a sharp iron knife and slit two buns, then delicately plucked two red, spicy-smelling sausages out of the cart with his fingers. He slathered them with mustard and ketchup and forked sauerkraut and fried onions on top of them. "There you go, miss. Don't drop 'em."

Violet had always been taught that only the very lowliest of the Wrong Sort of People ate on the street, and Myrtle had apparently been taught the same thing. They walked for a minute in silence, breathing the delicious smell of onions. Violet's stomach growled.

"In here," Myrtle said. They stepped into a narrow alley crisscrossed with clotheslines overhead and gobbled the hot dogs out of public view. Violet thought nothing had ever tasted better.

4

Henry Street

THE HENRY STREET SETTLEMENT HOUSE had stone steps with wrought-iron railings. At the bottom of the steps sat a group of girls playing jacks and a woman rocking a baby in a baby carriage with her foot. Violet followed Myrtle up the steps to a heavy wooden door.

"I think we just go in," said Myrtle.

Violet had a lifelong training in good manners, and it did not include going into other people's houses without knocking. She hesitated, but Myrtle pushed the door open and went in. Violet followed her with some trepidation. The house had an ordinary hall, with a carpet and an umbrella stand.

Upstairs, some people were singing. Violet couldn't understand the words. They were in a foreign language.

Violet looked questioningly at Myrtle. Myrtle shrugged. "I've never been inside here before," she said.

Violet went over to one of the doors and tentatively pushed it open.

It was a parlor, rather like the one back home had been before it was turned into Stephen's recuperation room. There were some bookshelves, a mahogany table, and a sofa and some armchairs covered in red velvet.

A man was sitting in one of the chairs, absorbed in a book. He had a thin, harried look, as if he hadn't gotten enough sleep in several years. Violet stepped hesitantly into the room. She could feel Myrtle following just behind her. "Excuse me . . . ," she began.

The man started, although Violet noticed he closed the book on his hand to keep from losing his place, just as she would have done.

"Good evening, ladies." The man stood up, as if Violet and Myrtle were in fact ladies. "How do you do?"

"Very well, thank you." Violet curtsied, and Myrtle did the same. All this politeness was such a waste of time—she just wanted to see her sister! "I was wondering if you might know where I can find Miss Chloe Mayhew."

As soon as she said Chloe's name, the man dropped the book.

He bent to pick it up, examining it carefully for damage. Violet wondered if he was going to answer her. She studied him while he wasn't looking. He was about as tall as Father, nearly six feet, but much thinner, and was wearing a ready-made brown suit and a soft-collared shirt that Father wouldn't have been caught dead in. In fact, Violet wasn't sure she had ever seen a man out in public in a soft-collared shirt. He had light brown hair that was just a little longer than it should have been, but the strangest thing about his face was an angry white scar that ran from the corner of his left eye down into his bushy mustache. Violet found it difficult to keep her eyes off it, though of course she knew that good manners required her to do so.

Finally he decided the book wasn't damaged. "I hope you ladies won't think me discourteous if I express some curiosity as to who might be inquiring for Miss Mayhew," he said. "Won't you please be seated?"

Violet sat down on the edge of the sofa that the man indicated. The cushion creaked as Myrtle sat down beside her. Violet wanted him to hurry up and go find Chloe for her. But of course it wouldn't be polite to say so, and Violet could see that this man was very polite. He spoke in the polite way that the boys had to talk to the girls at the dancing school that Mother made Violet go to, but unlike the boys at dancing school, he seemed quite comfortable doing it.

Violet glanced at Myrtle, wondering what she was making of the stranger. Myrtle raised her eyebrows in a sort of facial shrug.

"I'm Miss Violet Mayhew," said Violet to the man. "I'm Miss Mayhew's sister. And this is Myrtle, um . . ." She had forgotten Myrtle's last name.

"Davies," said Myrtle.

"And I am Theo Martin," said the man, sitting down.

"It's a pleasure to meet you." He clasped his book between his thumb and forefinger, and Violet realized with surprise that those were the only two fingers he had on his right hand. She looked quickly away and saw Myrtle trying not to notice the missing fingers as well.

"I'm afraid Miss Mayhew isn't here," said Mr. Martin. "She isn't in New York, actually."

Violet felt as if she'd just been punched in the stomach. That Chloe wouldn't be in New York was a possibility that hadn't occurred to her.

"But I have letters," she protested, starting to reach for them and then remembering that they were in her bloomers, not really a place you could reach for in a public parlor. "I thought she lived here." She could feel tears starting in her eyes and fought valiantly to keep them from spilling out. A lady never cried in public. She felt someone touch her and looked with surprise to see Myrtle's hand resting on her arm.

Mr. Martin leaned forward, looking concerned. "I'm sure your sister is in excellent health, Miss Mayhew; she's simply not in New York. Please don't worry."

Violet tried to smile to reassure him and accidentally jarred one of the tears loose. It trickled down beside her nose.

"She went to Washington, D.C., over a year ago to work with the National Woman's Party on the Susan B. Anthony Amendment. She drove off in that alarming machine of hers." He smiled fondly. "Chlo—Miss

Mayhew said that she loved nursing but that winning the vote for women was more important right now."

Violet had managed to get control of her tears. "Chloe's been a suffragist ever since she was in high school," she said. "Even then she worked on petitions and things."

"Well, it's a very worthwhile cause," said Mr. Martin.

Violet looked at him, surprised. "You think so?"

"Of course. Denying equal suffrage to women is a terrible injustice."

Violet was astonished. She had heard people say this before—Chloe chief among them—but she'd never heard a man say it. She hadn't really thought a man could want votes for women. Father certainly didn't. And none of the men from the bank that he invited for dinner, Mr. Russell and Mr. Rice and Mr. All-the-rest-of-them, did. As for Stephen—she hadn't really known Stephen that well; he'd been away since she was little, first at Cornell University and then at the War. For the last three years he hadn't voiced any opinions, even though Father had made Mother dress him up so he could take him to the polls to vote on Election Day just the same.

"My father says woman suffrage is a damn-fool crazy idea," Violet blurted, then clapped her hand to her mouth. "I beg your pardon."

Mr. Martin smiled. "Every great advance in human society started out as a damn-fool crazy idea."

"Er, yes," said Violet, feeling the conversation was getting off track.

Myrtle apparently thought so too, because she said, "Do you have an address for Miss Mayhew in Washington, sir?"

"An address? Now wait a minute. . . ." Mr. Martin put his book down. "Are you in New York with your parents, Miss Mayhew? And what about you, Miss Davies? Where have you sprung from, and don't they miss you there?"

Violet and Myrtle glanced at each other, alarmed. Mr. Martin had been speaking so normally that Violet, at least, had forgotten that he was an adult and likely to be interested in these sorts of details. She was trying to think of an evasive answer to this while still not looking at Mr. Martin's missing fingers or his scar when Myrtle said, "She just wants an address to write to, I think, Mr. Martin."

Mr. Martin still looked suspicious, so Violet hastily agreed. "Yes, just to write to. My father and mother don't . . . That is, they and Chloe had an argument. . . ."

Mr. Martin frowned. "And you, Miss Davies?"

The door opened inward halfway and a woman's voice called, "Theo! Come help me get these boys out of the chimney."

"Excuse me," said Mr. Martin, standing up again. "I'll just be a minute. Please wait right here."

As soon as he had left the room, Violet said, "We'd better go," at exactly the same moment that Myrtle whispered, "Let's get out of here."

Violet smiled in spite of her anxiety. She and Flossie used to say the same thing at the same time too. She looked out into the hallway. There was no sign of Mr. Martin or anyone else. They rushed out the front door, careful not to slam it behind them.

When they were out in the street again, Myrtle said, "That Mr. Martin was going to trot me over to the institute, and then put you on the first train back to Pennsylvania. What are you gonna do now? Should we go to Washington to find your sister?"

Violet had been thinking just that, though she had no idea how to get there. "Don't you have to go back to your training institute?"

"I told you. I try not to spend too much time there."

"But don't they want you there?" Violet still wasn't sure exactly what a girls' training institute was, but if it was anything like a school, they would.

"Yes," said Myrtle unconcernedly. "Do you have enough money for the train to D.C.?"

"I don't think so," said Violet. "How far is it?"

"A long way," said Myrtle. "More than two hundred miles."

Violet didn't have to do the math. At two cents a mile, she did not have enough money. "How will I get there?"

"We'll find a way," said Myrtle. "Let's go to the train station and see what we can figure out."

"But what about your school?" Violet persisted. She couldn't believe Myrtle was just going to wander away.

"It isn't a school," said Myrtle testily. "It's a training institute. A school would be a place where you learned stuff from books so that you could do something important in the world. My mama sent me to a school when she was alive. She didn't want me to go to someplace where we study ironing and dusting and knowing our place. Mama didn't mean for me to know my place."

Myrtle had started out this speech sounding cranky, but at the end there was a dangerous squeak in her voice, and Violet was afraid she was going to start crying. She never knew what to do when people started crying. Fortunately, Myrtle didn't.

"Come on," Myrtle said. "Let's go to the train station."

5

Hobie and the Brakeman

THEY WOULD NEVER HAVE GOTTEN TO WASHington if Hobie the Hobo hadn't shown them how to frisk a head-end blind. He was about Violet's age, she was sure. He wore knee britches and the same sort of ankle-high black boots that Myrtle and Violet had, but his face wore a studied expression of world-weariness that made him look at least forty. He had a plug of tobacco fixed firmly in his left cheek and talked around it in fluent hobo slang.

"You Angelinas lookin' to catch a blind?" he said as Violet and Myrtle stood on the platform in Penn Station, wondering what their chances were of boarding a train without tickets and not being caught.

"What?" said Myrtle.

"Are you blind baggage?" he said.

"Er, I don't think so," said Violet firmly, in an attempt to end the conversation. Hobie looked exactly like the Wrong Sort of People that her mother was always talking about.

"Too bad. You should be, if you want to make the miles. Hopping the freights is for rubes," said the boy. "Too slow—even if you get on a five-hundred-miler, who wants to spend all their time on the drag line? And you can get your legs sliced off riding the rods. You gotta ride the blinds, you wanna make any miles."

Violet moved away, but to her distress, Myrtle was looking at the boy with interest. "Can you get us onto a train?" Myrtle said.

"Thought you'd never ask, Angelina. Name's Hobie. Hobie the Hobo." He extended his hand.

Myrtle shook it. Then he stuck his hand at Violet. She wanted nothing to do with this boy, but she was too polite not to take his hand and shake it. His hand felt rough and callused.

"A lot of the brothers and sisters of the road won't come into the Big Burg," Hobie said. "Too many bulls in New York. But it ain't hard if you stay away from the freight yards and know how to catch a blind."

"We need to get to Washington," said Myrtle. "Can you show us how?"

"Washington." Hobie swept his hair back from his forehead and rocked back on his heels, thinking. "Gonna catch the Bum's Own, then the Ma and Pa. Those are railroads," he added. "Gonna change in Philly and Baltimore. Stay off the hot boxes unless you can catch a hotshot. . . . Aw, you Angelinas don't know anything about riding the rails, do you?"

"No, nothing," said Myrtle.

But it soon became clear that Hobie knew everything, at least about hoboing, and he intended to tell it to them. As he talked, Violet drew Myrtle aside and tried to whisper that they needed to lose Hobie, quickly.

Myrtle wouldn't even let her start. "He's going to help us," she said, shrugging Violet away.

Violet was annoyed. She didn't want to be thought a coward. She liked that Myrtle was a person who was willing to just take off and do something, like leave her school—institute—and go to Washington. It reminded her a little of Flossie, who was always ready to try something new without a whole lot of discussion and worrying and planning. Violet wondered if she'd changed so much since Flossie's death that she'd become a worrier and fraidy-cat that Flossie wouldn't even like anymore. It was a horrible thought.

She listened to what Hobie was telling them.

To be blind baggage meant riding in the blind spot between the engine and the baggage car of a passenger train. The trick was to duck in just after the highball—the two short blasts on the whistle that meant that the train was about to leave—and after the conductors had all stepped onto the train.

When the blast came, Hobie grabbed them each by a hand and darted onto the steel platform behind the engine so quickly that Violet caught her foot on the edge, stumbled, and almost fell onto the tracks. Hobie grabbed the collar of her middy blouse and pulled her back.

"Steady, Angelina!" he said.

They sat facing backward on account of the cinders, which flew back from the smokestack as the train gained speed and filled the air with the smell of coal smoke.

Violet and Myrtle sat huddled together, trying not to look at the ground whizzing by beneath them. The train jolted about as it picked up speed, and there was nothing to hold on to. The platform had no walls. One good jolt, Violet thought, and all three of them would fly off into the landscape that was zipping past.

Hobie was unperturbed. He leaned back and told them about his adventures. He was twelve years old, he admitted, and had been riding the rails on and off for two years.

"Where do you come from?" Myrtle asked.

"Tennessee. Copperhill, Tennessee. Up in the Blue Ridge. But there ain't hardly nowhere I ain't been," Hobie bragged. "Been all over Hobohemia." He swept his arm to indicate the scenery they were passing, which they couldn't see very well because they were squinting to keep the cinders out of their eyes.

It seemed to go on forever. What if she'd just stayed home, Violet thought—what would she be doing right now? It was night. She would have already read to

Stephen. Dinner would be over, including the nightly endurance of table manners and impossible rules (like eating everything on your plate, even horrible gristly fat pieces of meat, or you'd have to eat it for breakfast tomorrow). She'd be alone in her room, in her bed, under the green chenille bedspread, rereading one of her Oz books by the bedside lamp.

Instead, she was hunched over on the vibrating iron platform, breathing smoke and nearly deafened by the clatter of wheels on rails, so she could hardly hear Hobie. He seemed to be saying that he didn't need to go to school because he was going to be educated at some Hobo College that some rich man was starting.

It must've been nearly midnight, Violet guessed, when they reached Philadelphia. They walked across numerous tracks to a freight yard.

"We can catch a fast freight from here to Baltimore," Hobie said. "But it ain't here yet. I'm going over to the jungle to get some hobo stew." He indicated a clump of trees from which a thin column of smoke was rising. Violet and Myrtle started to follow him, but he held up a hand to stop them. "No, you Angelinas stay here. This is a bad jungle. Too many of the Johnson family, you know what I mean? Too many profesh."

"I guess he means criminals." Violet stopped and looked at Myrtle. "Oh no, do I look as bad as you do?"

"Probably," said Myrtle. "If I look that bad."

"You do," Violet assured her. Myrtle looked as

though she had taken a bath in charcoal. Her dress was no longer blue-and-white-striped but coal-smoke black, and her formerly white mobcap and apron matched.

They sat down on the gravel of the roadbed. It was very uncomfortable. Violet wondered if there was anywhere nearby where they could buy something to eat, anywhere that wouldn't mind serving people who looked like they had been swept out of the bottom of a fireplace. And if anyplace was even open at this hour.

"What time do you think it is?" Violet asked.

Myrtle shrugged. "Really late. I think it was around ten at night when we left New York."

Hobie brought them two tin cans full of what he said was stew. Violet was too hungry to be particular. They drank and ate the stew as best they could with their grimy fingers. It was full of vegetables Violet didn't recognize and bits of meat it was best not to examine too closely. But it tasted all right.

"We'll sleep here tonight," said Hobie. "But not in the jungle. I didn't tell the yeggs you were here—some of them don't know how to act proper around ladies. We'll sleep over there in one of them broke-down cars. There's a through freight to Baltimore tomorrow."

So that was what they did. Hobie told them more of his adventures as they fell asleep under a covering of newspapers on a wheelless flatcar. Violet looked up at the stars and wondered if she would really see Chloe tomorrow. When the newspapers fluttered and rustled in the breeze, she thought about her green chenille bedspread, but she didn't wish she was back in Susquehanna. She was having an adventure, and Myrtle was a good person to have an adventure with, just like Flossie would have been. It was funny, but Violet felt as if there was some part of her that had been locked up since Flossie's death—even more locked up than the rest of her was—and that it was being set free. As for Hobie, she was getting used to him. The main thing was not to look at him directly so that you didn't have to realize he was just a kid when he kept talking like he was his own grandfather. As Violet drifted off to sleep, Hobie was talking about how he wanted to go to Florida, one of the few places he admitted he'd never been.

It had been easy for Myrtle to decide to leave the Girls' Training Institute in New York. In her mind she'd left it the moment she arrived, a year ago, when she was nine. Myrtle didn't know where her life was going to take her, but she was ready for it to take her somewhere else, and she didn't intend to be anybody's maid.

Myrtle wasn't tough like Hobie, but she wasn't soft like Violet either. Still, she woke up in the morning stiff and achy. The rough wooden floor of the flatcar was even less comfortable than the lumpy cots at the Girls' Training Institute, which were said to be left over from the Civil War. She and Violet ate some stale doughnuts Hobie brought from the jungle and drank bitter chicory coffee from tin cans. Violet made a face over the coffee, and when Myrtle asked her if she'd never had chicory coffee before, she admitted she'd never had coffee before at all.

Hobie was wrong about one thing—boxcars were a lot more comfortable than riding the blinds. They rode in a deadhead (an empty boxcar) on the through freight to Baltimore. When they got to Baltimore, the railroad police (whom Hobie called bulls) chased them away from the blinds, so they had to take another freight. They were jouncing along in an empty boxcar, sitting on the wooden floor, watching tobacco fields pass by and listening to Hobie talk about the Rocky Mountains, when there was a loud wooden thump and a white man in a blue coverall landed on the boards in front of them.

Myrtle leapt to her feet and backed away from him.

His hands were balled into tight fists, and he advanced on them menacingly. "Stealin' rides, eh? Should I turn you in to the bulls or just throw you off the train?"

Hobie got to his feet and folded his arms. "It's your train, is it?"

"It sure ain't yours," said the man. "So what's it gonna be? Do I ditch you or are you ready to throw?"

"I don't have any money," said Hobie defiantly. "So ditch me."

The man clearly didn't like this idea. "How about one of the Angelinas, then?" He reached out and grabbed Myrtle.

He stank of sweat and soot. Myrtle struggled. His

hand dug painfully into her arm. He lifted her into the air and grabbed her ankle in his other hand. The floor and the walls lurched crazily past and Myrtle couldn't catch her breath to scream. He swung her—he was going to throw her out the open door.

"You ready to see her hit the grit?" The white man's voice seemed to lurch too. He swung Myrtle again—she saw the ground whizzing beneath her, terrifyingly close and fast.

"I have money!" Violet screamed. Myrtle saw a flash of grubby pink skin as Violet tried to grab the man's arm. "I have money! Put her down, right now!"

The man set Myrtle down, jarringly. If he hadn't been gripping her arms tight behind her, she would have fallen. "Mix me the hike, then," he ordered.

Violet scrabbled in her blouse and drew out a pinned handkerchief. She had started to hand it over when Hobie grabbed her arm. "Don't," he said.

"Are you crazy?" Violet snapped.

"Fifteen cents," Hobie said. "He gets fifteen cents."

"Thirty," said the criminal, twisting Myrtle's arms a few inches for emphasis. It hurt horribly. Myrtle felt dizzy with pain. She saw Violet wince with sympathy.

"Fifteen," said Hobie. "That's the hike."

"Ten cents per hundred miles," said the criminal. "Each."

"We ain't going no hundred miles," said Hobie. "We're going to Washington, and that ain't but half that.

Give him fifteen, Angelina." Myrtle couldn't believe he was arguing about money with this madman.

Violet handed the criminal three nickels. He grabbed them and let Myrtle go with a kind of disgusted shove. She fell on the floorboards.

"Are you all right?" Myrtle felt Violet's hands on her arms. "Myrtle, say something!"

Myrtle didn't want to say anything, because she thought if she opened her mouth, she might be sick. She wasn't normally a person to get dizzy easily, but then, nobody had ever swung her out the open door of a moving train before.

When she could see clearly again, the man was gone.

Hobie looked after him philosophically. "Don't think he's been a brakeman too long, that fella. You hardly ever see a braky who's still got both hands."

"A brakeman?" Violet stared at Hobie. "You mean that criminal works for the railroad?"

"Yup," said Hobie, casting a disgusted look out the open door.

"How . . . how did he get in here?" Myrtle asked shakily.

"Roof," said Hobie, nodding upward. "Brakies can climb all over the outside of a moving train, doesn't bother them none."

"I would th-think," said Violet, who Myrtle saw was starting to tremble now, "that they would fall off."

"Oh, they do. All the time. Die like flies," said Hobie.

"They're not all like that," he added fairly. "Most of them don't care if the brothers and sisters want to grab an armload of boxcars."

Myrtle had gotten used to Hobie's talk enough to figure out that that was another way to say "catch a ride."

It was evening when they arrived in Washington.

When they got off the train in Washington, Hobie stayed on it. "Think I'm gonna ride this as far as it goes," he said. "Might make it to Florida." He seemed to have no interest in actually *being* in any of the places that trains went to, Myrtle thought, but only in getting to them.

Myrtle had met kids like Hobie before. New York was full of them—grown-up kids who had been out on their own for years. She didn't really blame Hobie for being tough enough to argue with a brakeman who was threatening to throw her out of a train—toughness was what kept such kids alive. But the next thing he said shocked her.

"There are bound to be a lot of brakemen between Washington and Florida," Violet said. She reached for her pinned-up handkerchief of money and tried to give it to Hobie. He wouldn't take it.

"I have money," he said.

"You what?" Myrtle squawked. "You have money?"

"You were going to let that brakeman throw Myrtle out of the train when you had money to pay him with?" Violet demanded.

"No, of course I wasn't," said Hobie. He did not elaborate. "You Angelinas take care, now."

Myrtle didn't know whether to believe him or not—about the money and about whether he would have let the brakeman throw her off the train. She decided she had to believe he wouldn't have. The alternative was too awful. She took a deep breath.

"You take care too, Hobie," she said.

"Yes—and thank you," said Violet.

They waved to him as the train pulled out.

6

It All Comes Down to Tennessee

VIOLET COULD SEE THE HIGH NEEDLE OF THE Washington Monument in the distance as they picked their way across the gravel bed of the rail yard and stepped over rails and railroad ties. The smell of coal smoke and axle grease hung over everything. Rows of empty boxcars loomed on every side, and Violet could see smoke rising from a clump of trees where there must be a hobo jungle. It wasn't how Violet had imagined Washington would look. The important thing, though, was whether she would be able to find Chloe here. Violet was glad Myrtle was from Washington—she would know her way around.

"Do you know where to find the suffragists?" Violet asked Myrtle.

"Before we find anything, we better get cleaned up,"

Myrtle said. "Or anybody we find is gonna scream for the cops."

Myrtle led Violet out of the rail yard and down a cobblestone street with automobiles parked on it here and there. They turned down an alley and then down another alley that led off it. The alley was only just wide enough for a wagon to pass through. Brick and wooden houses lined both sides of it. The houses looked as if someone had built them in a great hurry fifty years ago and then fled. Probably to escape the fury of the people who had to live in them, Violet thought. The houses had no windows that Violet could see. To make up for this lack, there were a few holes where chunks of wall had fallen off.

Heaps of uncollected garbage overflowed from garbage cans and filled the corners, and the reek of rotten vegetables and mold mixed with a stench of raw sewage. A well-fed-looking rat ambled out from a pile of trash, looked at the girls thoughtfully, and waited for them to pass by.

"This isn't really how I imagined Washington," Violet admitted.

Myrtle smiled thinly. "No, they don't show this in the picture postcards."

Colored children lurked here and there in the alley, but they neither looked at nor spoke to Myrtle or Violet.

"This is where I used to live," Myrtle said. "It's called Louse Home Alley."

"Louse Home Alley?" Violet said, not sure she had heard right.

"Louse Home Alley," Myrtle repeated firmly. "Here's where we used to wash up."

Myrtle led the way down a narrow passage off the alley, which ended in a dirt-paved courtyard where a single water faucet came up from a pipe in the ground. There was a toilet of sorts, a shed that housed a long wooden box with holes cut in it. A horrible smell emanated from the deep pit beneath. Violet tried to pretend that this was nothing unusual to her, since her disgust was so clearly amusing to Myrtle. Violet liked Myrtle but wouldn't have minded if she were a little less of a know-it-all.

They ducked their heads under the faucet and scrubbed. Violet watched charcoal-colored water run down from Myrtle's hair and face, and she was sure it did from hers too. Myrtle took off her apron, revealing an apron-shaped area of blue and white stripes on her now black dress. She tossed the apron and mobcap into a corner of the courtyard.

"You're lucky your clothes were navy blue," said Myrtle.

She was right, Violet thought. The dirt didn't show as much. Score a point for Mother. Violet wondered if Mother was worried about her. Maybe she was just mad. It was an uncomfortable thought. Violet had never done anything as bad as running away before.

Coming out of the alleys seemed to take less time than

going in had. Soon they were on an ordinary street of ordinary brick houses. Two colored women sat on a set of stone steps, one of them rocking a baby carriage with her foot. Some boys played marbles. There were no heaps of garbage and no rats.

They turned into another street, wide and clean-swept and lined with tall brick houses with bay windows. Model Ts and some bigger, more expensive cars were parked along the street. "There's a suffrage lady who lives here," Myrtle explained, leading Violet up a set of stone steps to a brick house. She rapped on the door with a brass knocker.

The lady who opened the door was colored, with gray hair piled high on top of her head, and dressed in a blue brocaded dress with a high collar. There was something regal about her, Violet thought. She couldn't tell if it was the woman's bearing or her nose, which was long and had a royal tilt at the end. Probably both. The woman looked at Myrtle and Violet with a questioning eye.

Myrtle seemed momentarily abashed but recovered. "Ma'am, are you Professor Mary Church Terrell?"

"Yes," said the lady. "And you are?"

"Myrtle Davies, ma'am," said Myrtle. "And this is Violet Mayhew, and we're looking for the woman suffrage ladies."

"Indeed?" said Professor Terrell, raising an eyebrow at Violet. "Which women's suffrage ladies?"

"My sister came here from New York to work for women's suffrage," Violet said. "I think she's working on the Susan B. Anthony Amendment; do you know—"

"I am familiar with the Susan B. Anthony Amendment, yes," Professor Terrell said dryly. "I think your sister is probably with Miss Alice Paul and the National Woman's Party. Their headquarters is Cameron House on the west side of Lafayette Square, near the White House. Do you know how to get there?"

"Of course, ma'am," said Myrtle.

"Perhaps you'd better wash up a bit before you go," said Professor Terrell. "Good day."

They walked toward the Washington Monument, passing by more blocks of tenements and corner stores and then into neighborhoods with stately stone houses with broad lawns behind cast-iron fences. Wide avenues ran into other avenues in traffic circles that they had to walk around. There was more traffic now: motorcars, some of them Model Ts like the Hope Chest and some of them elaborate open limousines, Packards and Pierce-Arrows that could hold a dozen people comfortably. Dark green electric trolleys zipped down tracks in the middle of the streets. At some of the more opulent houses, guards in uniform stood at the doors.

"Those are foreign embassies," Myrtle explained.

It was getting dark when they got to Lafayette Square, a park surrounded by rather grand buildings and houses, one of which, Violet realized with a shock, was the White

House. It was set back a bit, behind a wide green lawn. People were strolling on the White House lawn.

Violet stopped to gaze at it. She had seen pictures of the White House all her life, of course, in her schoolbooks and on postcards and on the stereoscope, but now she was standing in front of it—the place where President Woodrow Wilson lived. Where Abraham Lincoln had lived.

"It's kind of small," she said at last.

Myrtle raised her eyebrows. "You think so? I wouldn't mind living there."

They crossed Lafayette Square to a wide three-story house that stretched between two bigger buildings that had electric signs identifying them as the Cosmos Club and the Belasco Theatre.

It was hard to believe that it was only yesterday morning that Violet had left Susquehanna; it seemed like a week ago. She wondered if Chloe could possibly be here. The place seemed so grand and un-Chloe-like. Chloe had always talked about living in a log cabin in Alaska. Violet reached up and pulled the door knocker.

"I'll get it, Miss Paul!" a voice said.

The door opened, and a young woman with bobbed brown hair looked down at them in surprise. "What on earth . . ." She stepped back and started to close the door.

Violet felt panic rising in her throat. Was she never going to find Chloe?

"I'm Chloe Mayhew's sister!" she cried desperately.

The door creaked open again. "Chloe Mayhew's sister?" the woman said.

"Yes," said Violet. "Is she here? I need to talk to her."

The woman frowned at Myrtle. "And this is?"

"I'm Myrtle Davies."

"May we come in, please?" said Violet. She knew this was rude, but the woman's expression suggested she was still going to close the door in their faces, and Violet had been through too much for that. She wanted to see Chloe, now.

"I suppose," said the woman, frowning at Myrtle.

They stood in the entrance hall while the young woman hurried away calling, "Miss Paul!"

Miss Paul meant Alice Paul, Violet realized with a jolt as the famous woman came out to greet them. Violet had heard of Alice Paul. Flossie had read about her in the newspapers, about how she had organized the nationwide fight for the Susan B. Anthony Amendment, about the women picketing in front of the White House and being attacked by bystanders and soldiers and finally being hauled off to jail. Flossie had made Violet read in the paper Miss Alice Paul's description of how she'd been force-fed by the jailers when she went on a hunger strike. Violet's throat had ached in sympathy for hours after she read it, even though she knew that Mother and Father did not approve of suffragists like Miss Paul. And Chloe. Violet had been annoyed at Flossie for making her read it. She would rather not have known about something that made her feel so uncomfortable.

Miss Paul was a mild-looking brown-haired woman of about thirty-five. She smiled questioningly at Violet and Myrtle. "Miss Mayhew's sister?" she asked Violet.

Violet nodded, not sure how you spoke to famous people.

"Her name's Violet," said Myrtle helpfully. "And I'm Myrtle Davies."

"Goodness. You'd better come in and have some tea," said Miss Paul.

Violet and Myrtle followed Miss Paul and the lady who'd come to the door, Miss Dexter, into the kitchen. Violet was conscious that her and Myrtle's shoes were tracking black train soot on the carpet.

"Your sister's been off campaigning for months," Miss Paul explained as she poured tea for them. "Ever since the amendment passed Congress with the required two-thirds vote. She took off in that flivver of hers—"

"The Hope Chest," Violet said, and then realized that she'd interrupted. "I beg your pardon, Miss Paul." But now that she'd interrupted, she might as well get to the important part. "Do you mean that Chloe isn't here?"

"No, she's in Tennessee," said Miss Paul.

Violet felt herself sag with disappointment. "Tennessee? Really?"

"Yes, that's where it's all come down to, and so that's where Miss Mayhew is." Miss Paul smiled. "She's a real fighter, your sister. She picketed the White House with us, and she went to jail."

"Jail?" said Violet, so surprised she forgot her disappointment for a moment. "Chloe?"

"Don't look so shocked, Violet!" said Miss Paul. "I've been to jail myself."

"I know," said Violet. "I read about it in the papers." She was getting the hang of talking to famous people now. Miss Paul was very normal-seeming and friendly.

"Not the *New York Times,* I hope!" said Miss Paul, smiling.

"Well, yes," Violet admitted. "My father made me read the one that said . . ." Violet saw from Myrtle's expression that she didn't know what they were talking about, so she explained. "The *New York Times* said that the women picketing the White House just proved that women were unsuited to voting, because no man would ever dream of picketing the White House." She turned back to Miss Paul. "My father liked that a lot, when they said that."

"Hello!" A woman with bright red hair came into the kitchen. "Did I hear you talking about jail? I've been to jail six times. We might as well have some of those biscuits if we're having tea."

"Girls, this is Miss Lucy Burns." Miss Paul told Miss Burns the girls' names as she opened a packet of Uneeda biscuits. "So your father liked the *Times* article? A lot of people did. I didn't care for it much." She laughed. "The *Times* has always been against us, but we've won New York anyway."

Miss Paul looked at the map on the kitchen wall and sighed.

Violet and Myrtle looked at the map too. Stars were penciled in on thirty-five of the forty-eight United States. Thirty-five states had ratified the Susan B. Anthony Amendment. Thirty-six were needed for the amendment to become part of the Constitution. If it did, then women would be able to vote in all forty-eight states, not just the sixteen states that had already passed woman suffrage laws of their own.

"Now it's all come down to Tennessee," said Miss Paul. "A lot of our workers have been there all summer. More are leaving in a few days. Miss Dexter's going. I had hoped to go too, but somebody's got to stay here and manage things at this end . . . keep pressure on the president, on both political parties, and on Governor Cox and Senator Harding. The two presidential candidates."

Myrtle got up and walked over to the map. She traced the states that didn't have stars with her finger. There were thirteen of them. "There are a lot of states here that could become number thirty-six," Myrtle said. "Why Tennessee?"

"Tennessee has agreed to hold a special session of their legislature to consider ratification," said Miss Dexter in a tone of voice that suggested that she still hadn't forgiven Myrtle for being in their kitchen. "North Carolina is holding a special session to take up a tax question, and they've decided to vote on ratification too. But we have a much stronger organization in Tennessee."

"Well, you're sure to get one," Violet said, looking at the long pink parallelogram of Tennessee, where Chloe was. "The other thirty-five came so fast." She remembered how the first thirty-five states had ratified the amendment, zip-zip-zip, one after another. Sometimes two in one day. She remembered Father and the Mr. R.'s grumbling about it at the dinner table and Mother clucking her tongue over what this world was coming to.

Miss Paul shook her head. "It's not that simple, Violet. You see, we haven't just been winning states, we've been losing them too." She nodded at the map. "While we were winning thirty-five states, the Antis won eight."

"Antis?" said Myrtle.

"Antis are people who are opposed to woman suffrage," said Violet. "Like my parents." Violet looked from the tiny star of D.C. across yellow Virginia to pink Tennessee and wondered how she was going to get there.

"That's right," said Miss Paul. "So there are actually only five states still left in play. If we win one of them, the amendment gets ratified; if the Antis win all five of them, the amendment will be defeated, and that"—she sighed—"will be the end."

"But they won't win all five, will they?" Violet said.

"Three of them are states the Antis have always told us they expected to win," said Miss Paul. "Florida, North Carolina . . . and Tennessee."

"Oh," said Violet.

"And Vermont and Connecticut have refused to hold special sessions," said Miss Paul. "The governors of those states are Antis, and the governor is the one who calls a legislature into session."

Violet thought that this was starting to get confusing. "But they'll vote on the amendment when they come back in their regular sessions, won't they?"

"Maybe," said Miss Paul. "There's a presidential election coming up in November, though, and I'd like to be able to vote in it."

Myrtle stared at the map in fascination and drew a line with her finger from Washington, D.C., to Tennessee.

"Now I really think the best thing to do with you girls is to put you in a bathtub. Don't you agree?"

Miss Dexter shot Miss Paul an angry look, but Miss Lucy Burns said, "I do. Come along upstairs, girls."

Myrtle and Violet were put into a spare bedroom once they were clean and robed in Miss Paul's and Miss Burns's extra nightgowns. In spite of how big the house was, they were aware that an extremely heated discussion was going on downstairs in the kitchen. Violet strained her ears but couldn't catch what was being said.

"I wonder what they're arguing about?" she said.

"Me, I expect," said Myrtle.

"Fine, don't listen to me." Miss Dexter's voice was suddenly clear; she must have stormed out of the kitchen into the downstairs hall. "I'm only saying that this is exactly the sort of gesture that loses us sympathy in the South."

The front door of Cameron House slammed.

Violet wondered if Myrtle could be right.

One of the many things that Violet had heard several times during her virtuous years of silence at the dinner table was that colored people were different. Yet in the last twenty-four hours of traveling with Myrtle, Violet had noticed that colored people were really not that different at all. She didn't mention this to Myrtle, who presumably already knew it, but to Violet this was something of a revelation. It was the first time that she'd ever discovered, all by herself, that Mother and Father were wrong about some things.

Chloe had discovered it a long time ago and told Violet about it, but that was Chloe. For Chloe to be right when Mother and Father were wrong wasn't that surprising. Violet had just never expected that she could be right too. Violet had always assumed that her own disagreements with Mother and Father were her fault and that Mother and Father (particularly Father) were bound to be right, just by virtue of being Mother and Father. Yet clearly they were wrong about colored people.

Myrtle was no different from most of the girls Violet knew, except for the minor detail that when they started out their journey, Myrtle's hair had been straight, but after she'd washed it under the faucet in Louse Home Alley, it had turned crinkly. And except that Myrtle had been sent to a training institute instead of a school.

Still, Myrtle was probably being too sensitive, Violet thought. Probably Miss Dexter was upset about something else.

Violet lay awake for a long time, wondering how she was ever going to find Chloe. Maybe the National Woman's Party workers would take her to Tennessee with them. She rolled over to ask Myrtle if she wanted to go too. But Myrtle had gone to sleep.

7

Heading to Nashville

AN ALARMING SIGHT GREETED VIOLET AND Myrtle when they came down to breakfast in the morning. Mr. Martin, whom they had left at the settlement house in New York, was quietly sipping coffee at the kitchen table with his hat in his hand. Miss Dexter was at the table too. They both turned to look at Violet and Myrtle.

"Good morning," said Miss Dexter. She said it with a somewhat martyred air. She pushed a plate of toast toward the girls. "There's coffee on the stove."

"Good morning," said Mr. Martin.

"Good morning, Mr. Martin," said Violet awkwardly. She'd thought that once they'd gotten away from Mr. Martin and his awkward questions about parents at the Henry Street Settlement House, that would be the end of him. That he would actually come after them hadn't occurred to her.

"You followed us here, sir?" said Myrtle.

"Not exactly," said Mr. Martin. "I came here to make sure you were still in one piece, yes. But I took the train from Penn Station. I'm not really sure how you got here."

"We hopped two freight trains and a blind," said Myrtle matter-of-factly.

Violet looked down at her shoes, expecting to be scolded. It was her usual lot in life. But if Mr. Martin thought he was going to make her go home to Susquehanna, he could think again.

Mr. Martin raised an eyebrow. "That's very dangerous, you know. Accidents happen to people jumping freight trains. I've seen people who have lost arms and legs."

Against her will, Violet found herself looking at Mr. Martin's hand with the missing fingers. She would have liked to have asked what had happened to them, but such a question was unthinkable.

"And what about your families?" Mr. Martin went on. "Did you think to tell them where you are?"

"I don't have a family," said Myrtle.

Mr. Martin turned his raised eyebrow on Myrtle, and Violet felt the need to back her up. "It's true, Mr. Martin, she doesn't."

"And what about your parents, Miss Mayhew?" Mr. Martin said. "I think they must be frantic by now, don't you?"

"No," said Violet. "They only care about my brother, Stephen. They think girls aren't good for much."

"They are your parents," said Mr. Martin. "It doesn't matter whether you're a boy or a girl; they'll be worried. As soon as you've eaten, we will go out and send them a telegram."

"I'm not going back," said Violet, starting to panic. "I want to go to Tennessee! I want to see Chloe." She had planned on joining the ladies who were going to Tennessee, if they would let her.

"Please sit down and eat, Violet," Miss Dexter pleaded. The way she said it made Violet realize that she might be causing a scene, and so she immediately sat down and did as she was told.

Myrtle sat down and reached for a piece of toast. She spread it with strawberry jam. "Don't you want to go to Tennessee, sir?"

Unaccountably, Mr. Martin looked embarrassed again. "Why would I want to go to Tennessee, Miss Davies?"

"Because history's going to be made," Miss Dexter said enthusiastically. Two pink spots stood out on her cheeks. "I'm going! I wouldn't miss it for the world. If Tennessee becomes the thirty-sixth state to ratify the Susan B. Anthony Amendment, and women get the vote, won't that be something, to say you were there and saw it?"

"Yes!" said Myrtle.

"I'd like to go too," said Violet. She wasn't a suffragist, but Chloe was in Tennessee.

"Well, so would I," Mr. Martin admitted. He frowned at Violet. "But we're still going to wire your parents as soon as you're done eating."

Violet stared at him, unsure what he meant. He couldn't possibly mean that he was going to let Violet and Myrtle go to Tennessee and in fact go with them.

"It's my duty, anyway, to see that you get there safely," Mr. Martin added. He sounded like he was talking himself into something.

Miss Burns swept into the kitchen, her red hair glowing in the morning light. Miss Dexter introduced her.

"So, you're the Mr. Martin we've heard so much about!" said Miss Burns.

Mr. Martin looked down at his coffee, coloring. "Nothing too bad, I hope."

"Very little at all bad," said Miss Burns, amused. "I understand you taught Chloe to patch automobile tires."

Violet looked at Mr. Martin in surprise. She remembered that from Chloe's letters.

"And now he wants to go off to Tennessee," said Miss Dexter. "Along with . . ." She frowned at Myrtle again.

"Well, we have space on the train," said Miss Burns. "Why shouldn't they go and see history being made? And see a certain suffragist," she added, looking shrewdly at Mr. Martin.

The telegraph office was three blocks down Pennsylvania Avenue. It had a strange smell of ink, old wood, and electricity. Mr. Martin got Violet a form. Violet stared at it, nibbling on the end of the fountain pen chained to the desk. Myrtle tried to look over her shoulder, but the desk was too high for her to see. Mr. Martin wanted to make Myrtle send a telegram too, but she was adamant that she had *no one* to send it to. Violet didn't tell Mr. Martin about the Girls' Training Institute, of course. That was Myrtle's business.

You had to pay for a telegraph by the word—and a great deal, though Violet wasn't sure exactly how much. It was much cheaper than a long-distance phone call, which only very rich people could afford to make, but it was still expensive. Now, what could she write without letting her parents know where to find her?

She dipped the pen into the inkwell set in the desk. *I am fine,* she wrote, printing each word carefully on the form. Then she saw a way to save a few cents and crossed out *I am* and wrote *I'm.* She tried to think of something else to say—How are you? But that was the sort of thing you wrote in a letter, when you weren't paying for every single word.

"Well, that won't break the bank," Mr. Martin said, looking over her shoulder. "But you can't use any punctuation marks, so contractions like 'I'm' are out. And up to the first ten words it's all the same price, forty cents."

Violet dipped the pen in ink again, crossed out what she'd written, and started over. *Mother and Father I am fine.* That was six words. She didn't want to tell them she was going to Tennessee—what if they notified the police to arrest her there? For the same reason, she couldn't mention woman suffrage. She had four words left. *Hope you are too.*

"You'd better sign it," Mr. Martin suggested. "The signature is free."

Violet wrote her first name.

"You're a woman of few words," said Mr. Martin. He took the form up to the counter, dropped a fifty-cent piece on it, and slid it under the brass bars to the clerk.

"I can pay for it," Violet said. She still had forty-two cents left.

"Allow me. It was my idea, after all." Mr. Martin smiled. "There's nothing wrong with going off to have adventures, you know, as long as you let your folks know you're all right."

This was not something Violet had ever heard a grown-up suggest before. "You must have had a lot of adventures," she said, and then winced at her forwardness.

He touched his scar and smiled again. "Yes, a great many. When I was your age, I walked from Pennsylvania to Long Island with Mother Jones, on her Children's Crusade. But my parents knew I was going."

"What was the Children's Crusade?" Myrtle asked as they went out to the broad, busy street.

"A march Mother Jones—she's a labor organizer, remarkable old lady—put together to draw attention to child labor. She took a bunch of us kids from the mines and mills, especially those of us with something to show for our work." He held up his hand with the missing fingers. "She got all our parents' permission, and we were all outfitted with a tin plate and a spoon. We walked up through Pennsylvania to New York City and then out to Oyster Bay, Long Island, to call on President Roosevelt."

"What did President Roosevelt say?" Violet asked as they stopped to let a large open-sided sightseeing bus, shaped like an overgrown rowboat, pass.

"He wouldn't see us," said Mr. Martin. "So we walked back again."

"Then it didn't do any good?" said Myrtle.

"Sure it did," Mr. Martin said. "We kids got out of the mills for weeks. We had a lot of fun on that walk, playing and running around like other kids, sleeping in barns and eating what folks along the road gave us. Mother Jones and her helpers taught us to read too."

"But President Roosevelt wouldn't see you," Violet reminded him.

"No, but thousands of people did see us. You can never know what seeds your words and actions might plant. We may get children out of the mines and mills in this country yet—it's only been seventeen years since our march." He smiled wryly. "Even when you don't win, you don't always lose. Remember that."

"Yes, Mr. Martin," said Violet politely. "It's a shame a woman like Mother Jones can't vote to change the child labor laws."

"Mother Jones doesn't want to vote. She's an Anti."

Violet looked at him to see if he was joking. "Doesn't want to vote? Why not?"

"That," said Mr. Martin, "is a mystery."

Everyone was very busy at the National Woman's Party headquarters in Cameron House over the next two days. They were much too busy to worry about where Violet and Myrtle had come from; everybody took it for granted that in some way they belonged to Mr. Martin, who was going to Nashville either to support the suffrage cause or to seek out his lost love—there wasn't really time to discuss which. Violet and Myrtle helped in the preparations for the trip to Tennessee. This involved a lot of copying down of addresses, sorting notebooks and law books, and laying in supplies of postage stamps and telegraph forms.

Miss Burns found a few adult dresses that could be cut down to size for Myrtle and Violet. She also found a frightful plaid school dress with a double row of fat black buttons down the front and a black patent leather belt three inches wide, which unfortunately fit Violet perfectly. Violet got a neck ache and a backache and felt like an old woman after twelve straight hours of sewing to make the dresses fit. She could tell from Myrtle's expression that she felt the same, but in the end they each had a pair of very serviceable dresses. Violet would still rather have had overalls, but the suffrage women had explained that you couldn't look strange when you were trying to bring people around to your point of view.

"That just gives them an excuse not to listen to you," Miss Dexter said. "You wait and wear overalls after we've won the vote."

She said this with a frown at Myrtle and then a sidelong look at Miss Paul. Violet and Myrtle knew what this was all about. Miss Paul had no objection to Mr. Martin, Violet, and Myrtle going to Tennessee, but Miss Dexter had an objection—specifically to Myrtle. Violet had thought at first that Myrtle was overreacting in thinking this, but now she saw that it was true.

"Don't you have people in Washington?" Miss Dexter had asked Myrtle, rather pointedly, at the dinner table the evening after they arrived. "Didn't you say you were from D.C. originally?"

"They're all dead, ma'am," said Myrtle. "Like I told you before. My mother died in the Influenza, and my father died digging the Panama Canal."

"Well, what about the people who sent you to school in New York?" Miss Dexter pressed, brushing past Myrtle's dead parents without comment.

"The church ladies that packed me off to the Girls' Training Institute?" Myrtle retorted. "Oh, right. I'm so grateful to them, ma'am."

"Miss Dexter, tell the girls about New Hampshire, where you come from," Miss Burns interceded desperately.

The long oaken benches of the waiting room at Union Station seemed to disappear in the enormous, echoing arched chamber.

"The waiting room is ninety feet high and was modeled after the Baths of Diocletian," said Miss Dexter.

"He must've been pretty dirty," Myrtle muttered, and Violet laughed. The hall wasn't dirty, of course—it was spotless.

"It is the largest railway waiting room in the world," Miss Dexter pointed out.

That perhaps explained why it seemed so empty, Violet thought. There were people in it, but they were dwarfed by the enormous arched ceiling. But most of the wooden benches were empty. Violet would have liked to get up and walk on them, turn at the curved seat at the end, and then walk back along the other side. But of course a young lady couldn't do that sort of thing.

The suffragists had rented their own train car, called a tourist car, which made the tickets to Tennessee much cheaper. There were some spare seats, because a few people—including Miss Burns and Miss Alice Paul—had decided not to go. The suffragists had agreed to take Violet and Myrtle and Mr. Martin along, and Violet had the impression that Mr. Martin had given them some money.

They were a jolly crowd boarding the train—even rowdy, Violet thought. Some wore sashes of green, white, and purple, or gold, white, and purple, or green and gold—all of these colors symbolized support for woman suffrage. Some of the women had badges and medals, and when Violet looked closely, she saw that some of the badges said that the women had gone to jail for the cause, and others said *Hunger Striker.* These were women who had picketed the White House in snowstorms, and been in jail, and starved themselves for woman suffrage. A group of them joined arms and sang:

Oh, we troubled Woody Wood as we stood,
as we stood.
We troubled Woody Wood as we stood!
We troubled Woody Wood,
and we troubled him right good.
We troubled Woody Wood as we stood!

"Don't sing that song!" a woman protested. "It was Woodrow Wilson who asked Governor Roberts to call this special session in Tennessee."

"Only because we troubled him till he did!" another woman called out, laughing.

The train rumbled to a stop, and the suffragists found their car and climbed aboard.

The conductor came along checking tickets and stopped when he got to their party. He stood over Myrtle, looking down at her disapprovingly.

"This won't do," he said.

Myrtle looked up at him, her face expressionless. The skirt of her blue dress was spread out on the red mohair seat, and her feet in their high-topped black shoes swung a few inches above the floor. He towered over her.

"What won't do?" Mr. Martin demanded sharply. He

and Miss Dexter were sitting on the seat opposite Violet and Myrtle.

"The colored girl. She's going to have to ride in the colored car."

"That's not the law in Washington," Mr. Martin said.

"Mr. Martin, please," Miss Dexter murmured.

"Well, it's not!" said Mr. Martin.

"Maybe not, but once we get moving, we'll only be in Washington for a few minutes," said the conductor. "As soon as we cross the District border, the girl needs to go in the colored car and stay there."

"But she can't ride by herself. She's just a child," Mr. Martin said.

The conductor shrugged. "She'll be among her own people. I'm sure they'll look after her."

Mr. Martin got to his feet, his face twisting into an ugly scowl that made his scar look more menacing. He no longer looked like polite Mr. Martin—he looked like some dangerous thug in a moving-picture show. Violet felt a lurch in her stomach. She had never seen adults fight before, and she didn't want to.

Violet looked at Myrtle and then at Miss Dexter. Miss Dexter was determinedly looking out the window. Violet looked back at Myrtle, who looked away.

Violet was sure there was nothing Mr. Martin—let alone Violet herself—could do; rules were rules. But it seemed really unfair to Myrtle. She reached out and took Myrtle's hand and glared at the conductor.

The conductor ignored her. "I'm sorry, sir," he said to Mr. Martin, not sounding sorry at all. "You can keep her in here for a few minutes if you want, but once we cross the District line, we'll be under Virginia law. It's my responsibility to enforce the law." He smiled thinly. "And to have anyone who doesn't comply arrested."

This last sentence seemed to deflate Mr. Martin, like an inner tube with a pin stuck in it. His face went from red to pink to pale, and his fists unmade themselves.

The conductor pressed his advantage. "The ticket discount is only on this tourist car, sir. It'll be two dollars extra for the child's ticket in the colored car. Or one dollar if she's under eight."

"I'm seven," said Myrtle. She held Violet's hand tightly but still didn't look at her—her eyes had been going from Mr. Martin to the conductor and back to Mr. Martin like someone watching a tennis match.

Mr. Martin reached into his pocket and pulled out a handful of change. He counted out four silver quarters. All the fight had gone out of him, Violet thought. The conductor pocketed the dollar and made out a ticket, looking victorious. He slapped the ticket down on the seat beside Myrtle.

"Hurry up, girl," he said. "This train's about to start moving."

Myrtle walked off down the corridor, her head held high. She did not look back. The conductor stalked close behind her.

Mr. Martin hadn't sat down yet and was trying to get

Miss Dexter to look at him. "Miss Dexter, I'd have thought, since the suffragists have taken the whole car, it would have been possible to argue that—"

Miss Dexter turned suddenly from the window and glared at him. "Mr. Martin, I'll thank you to refrain from making any more scenes between here and Tennessee. This may be just a tourist jaunt to you, but to us it represents the culmination of a seventy-two-year battle."

Mr. Martin glowered at her. Then the train started with a lurch that threw him into her lap.

"A thousand pardons, Miss Dexter," Mr. Martin apologized, getting into his own seat with difficulty. "I can assure you that I care every bit as much about the woman suffrage issue as you do," he added frostily.

"I find that very hard to believe," said Miss Dexter. "But if you actually care about the Susan B. Anthony Amendment, then don't jeopardize our chances by making ugly scenes about unrelated issues."

"It is not an unrelated issue!" Mr. Martin said heatedly. "It's all the same issue. If you can't see that—"

"You sound like a Bolshevik," said Miss Dexter, and turned pointedly to look out the window. Mr. Martin turned the other way and stared across the aisle out the opposite window. The other suffragists in the seats around them were all trying hard to look like they weren't staring at Miss Dexter and Mr. Martin. Violet felt extremely uncomfortable. This was going to be a long train trip. She wished Myrtle had been allowed to stay.

8

In the Jim Crow Car

MYRTLE HAD HER BUNDLE TUCKED UNDER one arm—the extra cut-down dress and a toothbrush and a comb that Miss Burns had bought for her. The only possession she really cared about she always carried in her pocket, like a talisman. It was a tiny tin-framed snapshot that Mama and Daddy had had taken the day they were married. Mama had come through clearly, looking just like Mama only not as tired as Myrtle remembered her. Daddy was mostly hidden. The flash powder had left a blurred spot in the middle of Daddy's face, so that she could only see the edges of it. She wished whoever had taken the picture had known this was going to be the only time William Davies's daughter would ever see him and had tried again.

Daddy had gone down to Panama to work on Mr.

Roosevelt's canal just before Myrtle was born. Then he had died, either of yellow fever or in a cave-in; the boss who wrote to Mama wasn't sure. So many American colored men died digging the Panama Canal, according to Mama, that the bosses couldn't keep track of them. Myrtle imagined that Daddy might have looked a bit like Mr. Martin, only much handsomer, and colored, of course. She liked Mr. Martin. He reminded her of Daddy somehow, which was dumb, considering Myrtle had never actually met her father.

The conductor followed Myrtle down the length of the train car to the vestibule between the cars, then said, "The colored car's all the way at the back," and left her. Myrtle struggled to open the door into the next car, the one behind the one that Mr. Martin and the other white people were in. The door wouldn't budge. She braced one foot against the side of the train car and hauled as hard as she could at the handle. The door opened and she stumbled backward but managed to recover and get through the door before it closed.

The next car was full of white people, and Myrtle hurried through it. Some of them gave her cold stares over their newspapers. One woman smiled at Myrtle and said to the man next to her, "They're so cute when they're little."

The train started and Myrtle fell down. Somebody laughed. Myrtle got to her feet, angry but schooling her face to perfect passive indifference. She made her way backward as the train sped forward. A conductor grabbed her arm.

"You're in the wrong car, girl," he said.

Myrtle gave him a vacant look. "I'm going to the colored car, mister."

"The Jim Crow car is in the back," the conductor said. He opened the door at the rear of the car and shoved Myrtle through it. "Keep walking."

The floor of the vestibule shifted and creaked under Myrtle's feet. The doors to the cars were even harder to open now that the train was moving. Myrtle found she couldn't open the next one at all, and against her will, tears of frustration started in her eyes. Then a white man came through going in the other direction and Myrtle was able to pass through. He didn't even see her. Colored people were completely invisible to some white people, Myrtle had noticed. If she worked at it, she could make herself even more invisible. It was the only kind of magic she knew how to do.

Finally she got to the colored car. It was older than the other cars, with an open platform at the end instead of a vestibule. That made the door the hardest of all to open, but a young woman sitting at the front of the car saw Myrtle through the window and came and opened the door for her.

This car was made all of wood, and the seats were covered with woven rattan instead of mohair. The people in the seats were all colored. Myrtle felt relieved, knowing that nobody in the car was going to give her evil looks over their newspapers. But there was a conductor at the end of the car, coming toward her. He was white, of course; all conductors were. He was taking tickets, reading them carefully, and snapping them neatly with his hole puncher. Myrtle felt for the ticket she had in her pocket and hoped that other stupid conductor hadn't made any mistakes on it.

Myrtle looked around for an empty seat. The car was very full. She saw a space next to an old woman—remarkably old. The woman looked almost too old to be human. She looked more like a very ancient tree that Myrtle knew of that grew in Anacostia, Washington. The woman was wearing the full, long skirts that had gone out of fashion before Myrtle was born.

The old woman saw her looking and patted the rattan seat beside her. "No one sitting here, child."

"Thank you, ma'am," Myrtle said. The rattan seat creaked as Myrtle sat down in the space between the woman's full skirts and the wooden wall of the train car. The seat had no springs, and Myrtle jolted with each clank of the wheels rattling against the rails. Myrtle had heard someone say that trains ran on paper-cored wheels, but she didn't see how a train could run on paper, and the wheels sounded like metal to her.

The conductor stopped in front of the old woman and held out his hand for her ticket.

"Where are we headed to today, Auntie?" he said.

The old woman murmured something in reply. Her voice was so weak Myrtle couldn't make it out.

"Change trains in Lexington, Auntie," said the conductor. He punched her ticket and reached for Myrtle's.

"Change in Chattanooga for Nashville," he said to Myrtle. She guessed her ticket was all right.

"Mrs. Merganser is my name," said the old woman, speaking quite clearly once the conductor had moved on.

"Pleased to meet you, ma'am," said Myrtle politely. "I'm Myrtle Davies."

They rode on in silence for a while.

"You have people in Tennessee?" Mrs. Merganser asked eventually.

"Yes, ma'am." Myrtle had never heard that she had people there, but there were people in Tennessee, no doubt, so it was possible that some of them were Myrtle's.

Mrs. Merganser seemed to accept this as reason enough for Myrtle's traveling. People sometimes sent their children on trains alone, because who could afford an extra adult's fare just to escort a child who presumably had brains enough to change trains by herself?

"How old do you think I am, child?" Mrs. Merganser asked.

"I don't know, ma'am," said Myrtle, thinking that the woman must be at least a hundred.

"I don't know either. I was born in Alabama a long time before freedom came. When I was no bigger than you, I was sold away from my mother into Georgia, and I never saw her again."

Myrtle kept her eyes cast down and listened respectfully. She had met old people who had been slaves before. None of them had been as old as Mrs. Merganser, though.

"My first baby was sold away from me when he was one year old. The second as well. Then my master died and left me to his brother in his will, along with some cows and a horse." Myrtle heard the sarcasm in the old woman's voice. "But my husband he left to another brother. So I lost him too. Do you want an apple?"

Myrtle felt derailed by the sudden change of subject. "Yes, ma'am."

Mrs. Merganser dug an apple out of her handbag, polished it against her skirt, and gave it to Myrtle. Myrtle was struck by how bright and smooth the apple looked against Mrs. Merganser's wrinkled old skin.

Myrtle savored the first bite of apple, crushing it between her teeth and letting the cider run over her tongue. Mrs. Merganser went on.

"After freedom, I searched for my first two children, but I never found them. I didn't look for my first husband, because by that time I was married again."

Mrs. Merganser looked at Myrtle sharply, as though daring her to say anything.

Myrtle said, "Yes, ma'am."

"Nowadays they'd call that bigamy." She shook her finger at Myrtle. "You can't marry another husband unless you divorce the first one or he dies. But back then it didn't matter. Colored folk marrying didn't matter any more than dogs or cattle marrying, in the eyes of the law."

Myrtle wiped apple juice from her chin with her sleeve. Mrs. Merganser shook her head disapprovingly and handed her a handkerchief.

"I had eight children before freedom and four after," she went on. "And only three are alive today, not counting the two I don't know about."

Myrtle tried to think of something comforting to say and came up with, "Pretty soon, though, ma'am, they're going to let women vote."

Mrs. Merganser shook her head in disbelief. "You think they're going to let us vote? Even if they do pass this amendment and let white women vote, you think they're going to let colored women vote? You haven't been listening to a word I've said, child."

"Yes, ma'am," Myrtle contradicted.

"You don't know much, child. I've just been telling you how I was sold and willed and bartered about like so much livestock, and you've got it into your head that white folks are going to let *me* vote?"

Myrtle said nothing. To say "yes, ma'am" again would, she felt, be pushing her luck.

"I guess you don't know," said Mrs. Merganser, "that these white people talked about amending this amendment of theirs. They talked about fixing it to say that white women could vote and colored women couldn't. They said that would make it easier to get the amendment passed. And I'll tell you something."

"Ma'am?"

"These white people were right. If they could've fixed that amendment to leave out colored women, it would've passed a long time ago."

"Yes, ma'am," said Myrtle. She didn't know if what Mrs. Merganser said about the amendment was true. She hadn't paid very close attention to the news stories about it. But she did know one thing. "I'm going to vote, ma'am, when I grow up."

Mrs. Merganser huffed derisively. "We're sitting here in this Jim Crow car because white people don't want to have to look at us when they ride on a train. And you think these same white people are going to let you pick their president for them."

Myrtle looked at the floorboards. Put that way, it did sound foolish.

"And if you live in Washington, D.C.," Mrs. Merganser added, "you can't vote anyway, man, woman, or child; white or colored."

"Then I won't live in Washington," said Myrtle.

"I think you must be the most stubborn child ever born," said Mrs. Merganser.

"Yes, ma'am," said Myrtle, glad they'd gotten that straight.

9

Mr. Martin's Escape

THE TRAIN CLIMBED STEEPLY UP INTO WHAT Miss Dexter said (when she started speaking again) were the Blue Ridge Mountains. But darkness had fallen, and the only thing Violet could see out the window was the reflection of the inside of the train car, two long rows of passengers, mostly women, on red mohair-covered seats, surrounded by their handbags, hatboxes, picnic baskets, valises, and traveling pillows.

"I hope you understand I'm not a *racialist*, Violet," Miss Dexter was saying as she unpacked fried chicken, biscuits, and apples from a picnic basket. "Mr. Martin doesn't seem to understand this. He doesn't seem to realize that with everything we women have worked so hard for in the balance, we can't be distracted by every little battle that comes our way."

Mr. Martin had gone to look for something for them to drink.

"Can I take some of this to Myrtle?" Violet asked, indicating the meal Miss Dexter was serving out. A few days ago she would have considered it the very height of bad breeding to ask her hostess for more food. But she was starting to realize that being well brought up had its disadvantages. It kept you from asking for the things you needed.

"Yes, of course," said Miss Dexter. "I certainly don't intend to *starve* the child," she added, wrapping some food up in a napkin. "Separation of the races doesn't necessarily mean inequality, Violet, it just . . ."

In honor of her newfound rudeness, Violet walked away without waiting to hear the end of this.

Violet worked her way toward the back of the train. There was no point in asking directions, she thought, on a train. She found the colored car all the way at the back. Clutching the napkin in her fist, she opened the last door and walked back through the aisle of colored passengers. She found Myrtle sitting next to an elderly woman.

"I brought you some dinner," said Violet. She held out the napkin.

"Thanks," said Myrtle. "Mrs. Merganser, this is my friend Violet."

Mrs. Merganser looked at Violet and nodded a greeting. Then she closed her eyes and seemed to fall asleep. Violet supposed she must be too old to stay awake.

"Can I sit down?" she asked. She felt uncomfortable being the only white person in the colored car, but she was tired of Miss Dexter and in no hurry to get back to her. And there was something she wanted to ask Myrtle about anyway.

"Sure." Myrtle made a space between herself and the window, and Violet squeezed into it. The rattan seats in the colored car were even more uncomfortable than the mohair-covered iron springs. Why didn't they make train seats out of something more comfortable?

"I think Mr. Martin might be on the run from the police," she said to Myrtle.

"Did you only just now figure that out?" said Myrtle.

"Well, when did you figure it out?" Violet asked, annoyed.

"First time I saw him, back in New York. When he jumped a mile when we came into the room."

Violet wasn't sure if Myrtle was telling the truth or was just trying to show how smart she was. Anyway, Violet had more pressing concerns. "But don't you think he might be a little bit *smitten* with my sister?"

"Yes." Myrtle frowned.

They sat in silence for a moment.

"Doesn't your sister know how to send a fella to the rightabout if he gets too fresh?"

"I guess so," said Violet. One way or another, Chloe had certainly sent the Mr. R.'s to the rightabout.

"Then I wouldn't worry about it," said Myrtle.

"But what about him being on the run from the police—we think?"

Myrtle did that shrug thing with her eyes. Apparently she didn't consider being on the run from the police a major character flaw.

"Well, he could be dangerous," said Violet. "He could hurt us."

"He hasn't hurt us yet, has he?" said Myrtle. Violet must have conveyed by her expression that this wasn't a satisfactory answer, because Myrtle added, "There are lots of ways to get in trouble with the law without hurting anybody, you know."

Violet did not know this. "Anyway, I think maybe she already sent him to the rightabout, and now he wants to try to get her to change her mind."

Myrtle nodded. She must have come to the same conclusion. "Maybe she'll want to change her mind."

"I don't think so," said Violet. "She doesn't want a—a gentleman friend. She sent these fellas back home in Susquehanna to the rightabout, and they were much better-looking than Mr. Martin."

"Looks aren't everything," said Myrtle sagely.

Violet was starting to get a prickly, uncomfortable feeling in the back of her neck. She turned around quickly. From the studied way that everyone was looking somewhere else, she was sure they had all been staring at her a second ago. "Am I not supposed to be in here?" said Violet.

"I don't know," said Myrtle. "Probably not."

Violet got up. Being out of place was unpleasant; it made your stomach hurt. She might as well go back and get her own dinner. "I'll see you later," she said. She turned to say goodbye to Mrs. Merganser, but the old woman was sound asleep. She must be too old even to talk anyway, Violet thought.

Just as she got back to the suffragists' car, the door at the other end of it snapped open and two men strode in. The men were dressed in black suits with starched collars that seemed to hold their chins up uncomfortably high. They marched down the car and stopped in the aisle next to Miss Dexter.

"Excuse me, ma'am," said one of the men. "Is there a man occupying this seat?" He pointed to the place Mr. Martin had just vacated.

"Yes," said Miss Dexter, looking surprised. "He's just gone to get drinks."

"Aha," said the man who had spoken, and the two men looked at each other and nodded.

Then they just stood there. As Violet came up to them, she could see this made Miss Dexter nervous. They made Violet nervous too. They had an official, police-like air about them.

"May I ask who you are?" Miss Dexter said.

"I'm sorry, ma'am, we're not at liberty to say," said the man who had spoken first. Then the train lurched around a bend and both men fell sprawling down the aisle, their arms and legs tangled together.

They picked themselves up with great dignity, as if they had meant to fall down. They made their way back up the aisle to Miss Dexter, gripping the edges of the seats tightly.

Violet didn't know who these men were, but she and Myrtle both thought Mr. Martin was running from the police. Mother and Father would probably have thought Mr. Martin was beyond the pale. But Myrtle liked him. Maybe he hadn't even really done whatever it was the police were after him for. Maybe there'd been some kind of mistake.

Violet made up her mind. Even if there hadn't been a mistake, she wasn't going to let the police catch Mr. Martin. She liked him. He talked to her like she was a person, and he'd stuck up for Myrtle too. Whatever else he might have done . . . Well, she just hoped it wasn't anything too horrible.

Violet tried to slip past the two men, heading the way Mr. Martin had gone to look for drinks. One of the men stepped in front of her, blocking her way.

"I'm just going to use the saloon," Violet said, with the most innocent look she could muster. The bathrooms on trains were called "saloons," for no reason Violet could imagine.

The man stepped aside and let Violet pass. Violet tried to walk calmly to the end of the car, gripping the backs of the seats as the train's movement threw her from one side of the aisle to the other. She opened the door with difficulty and walked nervously through the narrow vestibule. The four doors at its front, back, and sides rattled loudly.

She opened the door to the next car and managed to squeeze through it before it slammed on her.

A conductor stepped in front of her—not the conductor from Washington, but a different one. "Whoa, there, missy," he said. "You don't need to be running around between train cars like that. It's dangerous. Where's your seat?"

"There," said Violet, nodding to the car ahead. One thing her eleven years of life had taught her was that most males considered women and girls to be simultaneously mysterious and not very bright. So it wasn't very hard to lie to them.

The conductor looked over his shoulder. "Well, then how did you manage—"

"Excuse me," said Violet, and pushed past him.

She found Mr. Martin in a vestibule after she'd passed through four more cars. He came out one door as she was coming out the other. He had a brown bottle of root beer in each hand and one sticking out of each of his trousers pockets.

"Mr. Martin, stop," she said, holding up a hand toward him. She was out of breath from the effort of walking in the rocking train and pushing through the heavy doors.

Mr. Martin stopped and stood looking down at her quizzically. The train was chugging slowly up a steep grade. The jointed floor of the vestibule heaved and creaked under their feet, and they both braced their legs to keep from falling.

"There are some men back there," Violet said. "Looking for you. They're wearing tight collars, and they won't say their names."

Mr. Martin looked surprised at none of this. "Palmer agents. Did they ask for me by name?"

Violet had to think for a moment. "No."

Mr. Martin nodded. "Good. Don't tell them my name, please." He put the two bottles of root beer into Violet's hands. "Forgive my abruptness, Miss Mayhew, but I'm going to get off the train here."

"To what?" said Violet, not sure she'd heard him right.

The train had reached the crest of the hill. "You can tell them where I got off," said Mr. Martin. "In fact, you had better. Give my apologies to the ladies."

He opened one of the side doors of the vestibule and stepped out.

"Mr. Martin!" Violet gasped.

The side doors were for getting off the train—but getting off after it had stopped, of course. Violet didn't hear him hit the ground because the train was making so much noise. It was true it wasn't moving very fast, but she couldn't see what he'd stepped off into, and neither, she thought, could he. There might have been a three-hundred-foot cliff beside the tracks for all either of them knew.

She dropped the root beer bottles—one of them

shattered—and grabbed the handrail beside the still-swinging door. She leaned out as far as she dared. She felt a warm wind on her face and smelled pine trees and coal smoke.

"Mr. Martin!" she called.

The train crested the mountain and started downward again, picking up speed. Violet heard a door behind her open. A heavy hand landed on her shoulder and hauled her back into the vestibule.

The two men—Palmer agents, whatever those were—glared down at Violet. The one who had grabbed her barked, "What do you think you're doing, miss?"

"Where's Arpadfi?" snapped the second one.

Violet angrily jerked her shoulder free of the man's hand. "Who?"

"Arpadfi. Where'd he go? Did he jump?"

"I don't know what you're talking about," said Violet.

"Listen, miss, we're looking for Sandor Arpadfi. Scar on his face, one eye, missing three fingers on his right hand. Sound like anybody you know?"

"Three fingers?" said Violet, playing dumb. She watched the remaining root beer bottle rolling around on the floor.

"We're not going to get anywhere with this one," said the second agent.

"She warned him," said the first agent, pointing to Violet. He gripped Violet's arm, hard. It hurt. "Where's Arpadfi, girl? Don't play games with us. This is a criminal investigation of the highest order."

"Treason," the other agent said succinctly.

Violet felt a twist in her stomach—treason, she'd always heard, was worse than murder. But why should she believe these two idiots? She could make her own decisions about people. Mr. Martin didn't seem like a traitor to her. She glared at the agents and said nothing.

"He must've jumped." The agent who had hold of Violet's arm nodded at the side door, which was still swinging, opening a few inches and then gently slamming itself shut again. "I'm going after him."

The agent let go of Violet and kicked the door wide open. Violet could see the light shining out the train's many windows flickering over the ground moving by below.

The agent turned to the other agent. "Question the Suffs. See if you can get any of them to understand what 'accessory after the fact' means. Then get off in Roanoke and cable J. Edgar Hoover that we've spotted Arpadfi." He stepped out through the door.

"No!" Violet cried, horrified, as he jumped. The train was by no means moving as slowly as it had been when Mr. Martin jumped off.

"Come on, miss," said the other agent, grabbing her arm. "Let's see what you and the Suffs can manage to babble out."

"You know, I don't believe he ever told us his name," Miss Dexter said loudly. Violet was surprised at how well she pretended to be stupid—and surprised she was willing to do it for Mr. Martin, whom Miss Dexter clearly disliked. "He joined us at Union Station and begged a spare seat in our car. But he's a complete stranger to me."

The agent, who had finally admitted that his name was Mr. Christopher, had sat down in Mr. Martin's empty seat and unfolded a paper on his lap—a rough pencil sketch that could have been Mr. Martin in the same vague way that pictures of Uncle Sam could have been Violet's Grandfather Mayhew. It did have a scar on it.

Many of the other suffragists had gotten up and crowded around, clinging to the backs of the seats for balance.

"Miss Dexter," Mr. Christopher said, "try to get this through that female wool you call a brain." (The suffragists hissed.) "This man is dangerous. He poses a threat to the United States of America. By helping to conceal him, you could be guilty of treason."

"What's he supposed to have done?" demanded a gray-haired suffragist in a purple dress.

"I can't tell you that," said Mr. Christopher.

The woman in purple snorted.

Mr. Christopher asked a number of questions, about whether anyone had heard Sandor Arpadfi mention where he had been, or where he was going, or any names of friends or relatives or associates. Nobody offered him much help.

"Did he say anything that sounded Bolshevist?" Mr. Christopher finally demanded. "You know, anything un-American?"

Miss Dexter shrugged delicately. "I suppose some of the things he said were a bit *socialist,*" she said. "But there's an enormous difference between a Bolshevist and a socialist."

"That's what the socialists would like you to think," said Mr. Christopher.

"Socialists are good Americans!" said the woman in purple angrily. "They believe in cooperation instead of competition. Many of the greatest and wisest people in our country are socialists."

Mr. Christopher sneered. "That's why women shouldn't be allowed to vote," he said. "The female mind isn't capable of making fine distinctions of logic."

The woman turned as purple as her dress. "Miss Helen Keller is a socialist!" she stormed. "Miss Lillian Wald is a socialist! Miss Jane Addams is a socialist! Miss —"

"If they kept their addled brains out of politics, maybe someone would marry them," Mr. Christopher said nastily. He got to his feet. The train was slowing as if approaching a station, but Violet thought that wasn't the only reason he was leaving. The crowd was closing in on him. Mr. Christopher took his pencil sketch and his notebook and retreated.

"What a horrid man," Miss Dexter said. The other suffragists agreed heartily. They made their way back to their seats, and Violet could hear them talking—speculating, she supposed, about Mr. Martin and what he'd done to get those dreadful government agents chasing him. Violet's stomach squirmed. She hoped the ground hadn't been too far away when Mr. Martin had hit it. Where had he landed, and what would he do now?

Violet looked over at the woman in purple. There was an empty seat next to her. Violet got up and jostled over and sat down in it. "Excuse me, Miss . . ."

"Kelley," said the woman, sticking out her hand and smiling. Fortunately, Miss Kelley didn't seem to know that children should speak only when spoken to. "Florence Kelley. Pleased to meet you."

Violet shook hands and introduced herself. "What are Palmer agents, Miss Kelley?"

Miss Kelley frowned. "Is that who those clowns were? I thought that might be it. Mr. Palmer is the U.S. attorney general, and he's got a crazy assistant named J. Edgar Hoover." Miss Kelley rolled her eyes at the ridiculous name. "Their agents track down radicals and arrest them."

"Arrest them for what?" said Violet.

"Mostly for being against the War," said Miss Kelley.

"But the War is over," said Violet.

"Parts of it are," Miss Kelley said.

"And what are Bolshevists?" Violet asked. She had some idea, but she wanted to hear what Miss Kelley would say, especially since Miss Kelley was clearly one of those rare adults, like Chloe and Mr. Martin, who talked about things that mattered and let you ask questions.

"The Bolsheviks are the people who overthrew the czar in Russia," said Miss Kelley. "But people just use the word to mean anybody that wants to change the way things are—to make us sound dangerous. Some people say we suffragists are Bolsheviks."

Violet nodded. She had heard that.

"How is your little friend in the Jim Crow car?" Miss Kelley asked.

Violet looked at her, surprised.

"She's all right," she said. "The seats aren't so nice there, but she's—fine." Violet didn't think it was fine at all, actually, but Miss Dexter had seemed to and she was an adult.

"It's a national shame," said Miss Kelley. "This Jim Crow business. My organization, the National Association for the Advancement of Colored People, is fighting to put an end to it. There's no reason decent people can't ride in a train car with each other."

Violet stared at Miss Kelley. "But you're not colored," she said. Then she covered her mouth, shocked at her own rudeness.

"No, I'm not, but that doesn't mean I can't fight for justice side by side with colored people." Miss Kelley patted Violet on the shoulder. "You know it's wrong, putting your friend in another train car. When you know right from wrong, don't let anyone tell you differently."

They both looked over at Miss Dexter.

"I won't, Miss Kelley," said Violet, and meant it.

Soon it was time to fold down and rearrange the seats into berths. A porter came in to help them with this.

Violet climbed into a top berth beside Miss Dexter. She lay awake for a long time, boxed in by the train's curving metal ceiling, the wall, the thin lumpy mattress, and Miss Dexter. She thought about Myrtle in the Jim Crow car, probably sitting up all night in that rattan seat. Finally Violet drifted off to sleep and dreamt that she was running and running, trying to catch a train that had left a long time ago.

Sometimes the train stopped at stations and Violet woke, sliding forward as her head bumped against the partition. Then she fell back asleep until the train started again and her feet hit the partition at the other end. The train whistle let out a long, loud moan each time the train came to a crossing. Finally Violet gave up sleeping and lay awake wondering what Mr. Martin had done to get people called Palmer agents after him and whether he had survived his leap into the dark.

10

Red and Yellow Roses

"DO YOU REALIZE THAT THE CHILD BORN IN 1920 will never know war?" Miss Dexter asked.

It was morning, and the Suffs were cooking oatmeal over the tiny cookstove at the end of the tourist car while the car changed trains at Chattanooga. Since the Suffs had rented the whole car to go to Nashville in, they didn't have to get off and change trains at the junction points. Instead, the car itself was unhitched from one train, rolled into a siding, and hitched up to another train.

"The Great War that ended in 1918 was mankind's last war," Miss Dexter went on. "We have a League of Nations now. More than twenty countries have joined it already. In the future all difficulties between countries will be arbitrated by an international court of justice."

Outside on the platform, a newsboy called, "Extra! Russians surround Warsaw! Riots in Ireland! English impose martial law!"

Violet wondered why Miss Dexter was able to imagine such a perfect world and not imagine a place for Myrtle in it. She got up and went over to the stove. Miss Kelley was glopping oatmeal into tin bowls. "Can I have some to take to Myrtle, please?" Violet asked.

"Here you go." Miss Kelley handed her a bowl of thick gray oatmeal. Then she reached into a box and heaped a liberal handful of raisins on top. "Better give her some extra; injustice makes a girl hungry."

Violet had to get off the train in order to find the car Myrtle was in—they were no longer connected. Everything was being rearranged so new trains could be assembled to head to Nashville and other cities from the junction point here in Chattanooga.

She found Myrtle standing on a platform on the other side of the tracks, in a knot of colored people who were waiting to get onto the Jim Crow car to Nashville. Violet hurriedly told Myrtle about what had happened the night before, but there was no time to discuss what might have become of Mr. Martin because Violet was supposed to get back to the suffragists' car before it was moved.

"Anyway, I'll see you in Nashville," she said, and hurried away to eat her own breakfast.

As she was crossing the tracks, she saw a woman carrying a basket stumble and fall.

Violet hurried over to help the woman up. She was tall

and angular and bony and, Violet saw with embarrassment, in an interesting condition. Violet could feel her face burn. Ladies who were about to have babies, at least as soon as this woman seemed about to have a baby, usually stayed home.

Violet picked up the lady's basket and also a scrap of black cloth that had fallen on the tracks. "Let me carry this for you," she suggested.

"Thank you, child." The woman put her hand on the small of her back and winced painfully. "I'm just going over to the platform to set down. Goodness, that hurt. Doesn't seem to have done any harm to the little one, though. He's still kicking away."

Embarrassed by this forthright talk, Violet carried the basket and the cloth across the tracks and up onto the platform. It was a picnic basket, but it looked to her like there were folded clothes in it.

The woman sat down painfully on a bench, still holding her back. "Thank you, child. Just put that down right here. That's my son's uniform. They're sending him home from France. He's supposed to be shipped to Chattanooga today."

Violet thought that was a funny way of putting it, and then she looked at the piece of black cloth in her hand and a thought struck her.

"Is your son . . . Did he . . ."

"Yes," said the woman. "Put that on my arm, would you, dear? It's supposed to be my mourning."

The War had ended almost two years ago, but

American soldiers' bodies were still being shipped home from France. It was a slow process, apparently. Violet shook out the black cloth and folded it diagonally, then again to make an armband. She wrapped it around the woman's gray calico sleeve. She could see in the seam that the calico had once been dark blue, but it was faded and worn whisper-thin from many washings. She tied the armband neatly.

"Thank you. Ow." The woman winced and put her hand on her belly, and Violet looked at her, worried. The woman's face was drawn and gray, and a strand of gray hair hung damply down from under her straw hat. Violet had never understood the phrase "hatchet-faced" before, but now she did—the woman looked as though her face had been cut out of a block of wood with a hatchet. It was all sharp, hard angles.

"Are you going to be all right?" Violet asked.

"I don't know," said the woman. "You know, child, if men knew how much work it is having babies, I'm not sure they'd be quite so willing to start wars and have our babies blow each other up."

"My brother was in France too," Violet said. "But he came back," she added apologetically. "With shell shock. He never talks anymore."

The gray lady nodded. "I hope the good Lord will grant that this is my last one," she said, resting both hands on her swollen belly. "And that no one dreams up a war to take this one away from me."

Violet was just about to repeat what Miss Dexter had said, that the human race had outgrown war, when a barefoot newsboy thrust a newspaper at them and hollered, "Extra! Russians surround Warsaw! Poland under siege! Warsaw to fall by the weekend!"

Miss Dexter was wrong, Violet thought, about a lot of things.

"If you could vote," Violet said, "then you'd be able to vote against wars."

"Vote?" The woman looked as surprised as if Violet had just suggested she tap-dance. "My husband would never allow that."

Violet was about to answer when a loud clang made her look up, and she saw that the Suffs' tourist car was being hitched onto a train.

"Excuse me!" she cried. "That's my train. Goodbye!"

She waved and hurried to clamber back aboard before they left without her.

As the train pulled out, Violet looked back. She could see the hatchet-faced woman sitting beside her basket, an angular gray figure growing smaller in the distance, until the train rounded a curve and she disappeared. Violet wondered what it would be like to be waiting for your son to come home from France in a box. She thought about the woman giving birth to her son (Violet's mother had told her that babies were brought by a stork, but Flossie had given Violet a different explanation that sounded only slightly less unlikely), and then changing his diapers and teaching him table manners and sending him off to school and making beef tea for him when he was sick, and then being told by the government that she had to send him off to France so that he could come home in a box.

The more Violet thought about it, the angrier she got.

Suddenly Violet understood why all these women were riding to Nashville on a train. It was so that women would never again have to sit by in silence while men made decisions they didn't like—whether it was Father deciding that Chloe couldn't go to college or the government deciding that people's sons had to go fight in France whether they wanted to or not.

The train pulled into a small station, a flag stop. The little covered platform was a jumble of trunks, porters, and valises. Men and women in stiff-looking best clothes milled about waiting for the train doors to open. Another newsboy who looked about eight years old was hawking papers, screaming at the top of his lungs, "Riots! Riots in Ireland!" Then, when that didn't attract any customers, "Tigers beat Yankees!"

Miss Dexter stood up and waved out the open window. "Paper!" she called.

The boy came over and handed a paper through the window. Violet could smell the fresh ink. Miss Dexter dropped three pennies into his outstretched hand.

The train doors had opened, and a few people went down the steps onto the wooden platform. Violet stared. If she hadn't known better, she would have sworn one of the people who got off the train was Mr. Martin. She looked again. It *was* Mr. Martin.

But how was that possible? Mr. Martin had jumped off a completely different train the night before.

She hardly had time to wonder before she noticed someone following Mr. Martin . . . or that's what it looked like, anyway. It wasn't one of the agents from last night, but the man wore a starched collar—of course most men did—and he walked with a speed and sense of purpose that seemed out of place on a railroad platform.

Violet sprang to her feet. She started up the aisle toward the exit. Maybe there was time, before the train left, to warn Mr. Martin he was being followed.

She was in the vestibule when the train started moving. She pushed at the exit door, but it wouldn't open. She gave it a hard push, and it came open, just as a hand grabbed Violet from behind.

"Let me go!" She hit out at whoever was holding her.

On the platform, she saw a small colored girl running toward Mr. Martin. She couldn't see if it was Myrtle; the train was already picking up speed, and the station was soon out of sight.

The conductor let go of her. "I don't know what you're playing at, missy," he said disagreeably, "but you're a Nashville passenger and to Nashville you're going."

Violet hadn't wanted to get off, only to make sure Mr. Martin knew he was being followed. But it was no business of the conductor's. "I can get off the train if I want to," she said angrily.

"Why would you want to?" the conductor said. "You're paid through to Nashville." He opened the door to the suffragists' car. "Now get back to your seat, miss."

In Nashville an army of women greeted the train, their arms full of flowers. They swarmed among the men and women getting off the train, thrusting yellow and red roses at them.

Violet stepped off onto the platform, holding the small bundle that contained her spare clothes. The train had pulled into a huge train shed with a high, soaring roof that covered all of the rows of tracks and platforms. Violet had never seen anything like it, but she didn't have time to study it. She looked along the train, searching for the colored car. There it was, all the way at the back. Violet hurried over to where colored men, women, and children were getting down from the two exits, carrying valises.

She watched every single person get off the colored car, but she didn't see Myrtle. So it must have been Myrtle who had chased after Mr. Martin this morning. And then what had happened to them? Had the Palmer agent caught Mr. Martin? If he had, then what would happen to Myrtle?

Violet paced anxiously back and forth on the platform, staring at the train and willing it to produce Myrtle. But it didn't, of course. Violet didn't know what to do. She and Myrtle had run away together—it was a joint project, and it felt wrong to have gotten separated from her. Besides, she was older than Myrtle and ought to have looked after her better. She went into the train station, worrying.

The station was even fancier than the one in Washington, though not as big. It had a high, arched stained-glass ceiling and mosaic tiles on the floor. A woman with a basket of red roses assailed Violet.

"Wear a red rose," she commanded, smiling sweetly and holding one out to Violet.

Violet took it uncertainly. "How much are they?" She didn't want to buy one but wasn't sure how to say no politely.

"They're free, dear. We just want everyone to wear a rose to show her support for the cause."

"Oh. Er, thank you." The stem was wrapped in paper tape with a long pin like a hat pin through it. The woman helped Violet pin it to the collar of her dress. Violet's eyes wandered over to a set of windows at the side of the grand room, which had a sign on them that said *Colored Waiting Room*.

"There!" said the woman. "Now you look lovely. Where are you staying, dear?"

"Er, with my sister," said Violet. A group of suffragists, some from the train and some who had greeted it, had joined arms in the middle of the mosaic floor and were doing a little dance, singing.

Oh, dear, what can the matter be?
Oh, dear, what can the matter be?
Oh, dear, what can the matter be?
Women are wanting to vote!
Women have husbands; they are protected.
Women have sons by whom they're directed.
Women have fathers; they're not neglected.
Why are they wanting to vote?

Violet did not see Miss Dexter in the circle, but she wouldn't mind losing her—she who had worn thin on better acquaintance. She didn't see Miss Kelley anywhere.

"I'm Miss Charlotte Rowe," the woman said, extending her hand.

"Miss Violet Mayhew," said Violet, shaking hands.

"Is your sister staying with us at the Hermitage Hotel?" Miss Rowe said. "I don't recognize that name, Mayhew. Or is your sister a married lady?"

"No, she's not married," said Violet.

"I'm surprised she didn't meet you at the station."

"She didn't know what train I was coming on," Violet said, which wasn't exactly a lie.

"Well, come along with me to the Hermitage," said Miss Rowe. "We'll get it all settled there."

Violet could think of no better plan. She was worried about Myrtle—and about Mr. Martin, of course—but she might be just moments away from finding Chloe at last. Chloe would know how to go about finding Myrtle. Chloe would make everything all right.

Violet followed Miss Charlotte Rowe, who handed her basket of red roses to another lady and said that she was leaving. They went out to a darkening city street, lit at intervals by globe-shaped streetlamps. A tired-looking horse clopped along, pulling a wagon with *Overton and Bush—ICE* painted on the side. They crossed the street, stepping around horse manure and over streetcar tracks, and turned down another street. They passed movie theaters and vaudeville theaters and drugstores, which, even though they were closed, advertised the fact that they had soda fountains with fountains formed of electric lightbulbs blinking on in succession, to look like streaming water. Well, sort of like it.

Violet was surprised to see such a lively, modern city, after the quiet towns and vast wooded mountains they had passed through on the train. Unfortunately, Nashville also seemed to be a very hot place, even at night. Violet could feel sweat trickling down her back inside her undervest.

"I know it looks quiet," said Miss Rowe. "This is the still before the storm, as they say. There's a battle brewing that's unlike anything the South has seen since the Civil War." She smiled grimly. "I'm from up north, as I gather you are too, Miss Mayhew?"

"Yes, Pennsylvania," said Violet.

"A state we fought long and hard for! Well, we have a

battle on our hands here, Violet. The other side is pouring every effort into Tennessee. They've sent in some of their most unscrupulous . . . Ah, here we are."

The Hermitage Hotel was ten stories high and mobbed, the crowd pouring out the grand entryway onto the street. Violet started toward the entrance, but Miss Rowe pulled her arm. "The ladies' entrance is around the side, Violet."

They went around the corner, under a vertical sign that reached up the side of the building and spelled out *Hermitage* in electric lightbulbs.

They went in through the much smaller ladies' entrance, then down a hallway and past the elevators to the lobby.

There was a crowd of men and women around the elevators, and a lady in a pink satin dress called out, "Charlotte! Come here a minute." Miss Rowe went to the lady, and Violet wandered on into the lobby.

The lobby was as crowded as the train station had been. Violet looked up at a high stained-glass skylight (which was dark now) set in an elaborately decorated ceiling, with plaster bosses and garlands of fruit. There was a balcony, and people crowded along the railing, looking down at the people in the lobby. Violet couldn't hear what anyone was saying—the babble around her was too loud, with hundreds of voices echoing off the marble floors and walls. In fact, she was getting an awful headache.

Violet looked around and found the registration desk. She made her way through the crowd of people in yellow roses and red roses and past an old man wearing what she thought was a Confederate army uniform. The desk clerk didn't seem to notice her.

"I beg your pardon—" she ventured.

"No rooms!" said the desk clerk, looking up. "I have no rooms left. Small or large. With or without conveniences. No rooms for Suffs, no rooms for Antis, no rooms for the Southern Women's Rejection League, the Men's Ratification Committee, the Tennessee Constitutional League, the National Woman's Party, the League of Women Voters, the Confederate Widows' Society, or the Women's Christian Temperance Union."

"I'm not with any of those," Violet said hurriedly. "I was wondering if—could you tell me if my sister is staying here? A Miss Mayhew."

"Suffs are on the third floor," the clerk went on, seeming not to have heard her. "Antis are on the seventh and eighth. Anti headquarters are on the mezzanine. Mrs. Carrie Chapman Catt and Mr. Joe Hanover are on the third floor although not, of course"—he sniffed delicately—"together. Miss Josephine Anderson Pearson is on the seventh floor. Antis' hospitality suite is on the eighth floor. People who take both the Antis' and the Suffs' side—"

"Mr. Walker!"

Violet turned. A woman was calling to a man in a

black suit who seemed anxious to avoid her. She called his name again and he turned reluctantly to face her. She looked very angry.

"Who got to you?" she demanded. "How much did they pay you, Mr. Walker? Was it thirty pieces of silver?"

Silence fell in the crowded room. Everyone drew back and watched. Mr. Walker put his hand to his throat and took a step back, looking shocked.

"Was it the Louisville and Nashville Railroad that bought you off, Speaker Walker?" the woman hissed.

"How . . . how dare you!" Mr. Walker jammed his panama hat on his head, spun on his heel, and stalked out of the hotel.

People started talking again, a little nervously.

"Huh," said the desk clerk. "That's the Speaker of the Tennessee House, Seth Walker. He was one of the Suffs' strongest supporters. If he's turned coat, I don't see how they can win."

"You mean he changed sides?" said Violet.

"So it would seem," said the desk clerk. "Interesting." He dipped his pen in ink and made a little note on his desk blotter, which Violet saw was covered with tally marks.

"Is there a Miss Mayhew staying at the hotel?" she repeated.

The clerk opened his ledger and ran his finger down it. "No, I don't have any Mayhew. Is she a Suff or an Anti?"

"There you are, Violet!" Miss Rowe came bustling up. "Did you find your sister?"

"She's not here," said Violet, feeling desperate. She had lost Myrtle and Mr. Martin and she couldn't find Chloe. She was completely alone. She felt like crying.

Miss Rowe looked unconcerned. "Squeeze her into one of our rooms for tonight, Frankie. Put her in with Miss Escuadrille; there's an extra bed in there. Violet, come down to the mezzanine once you get settled. You can meet some of the really important leaders in our movement, like Miss Josephine Anderson Pearson! Oh, there's Mr. Burn—I must speak to him. Excuse me."

Violet looked back at the desk clerk. He ran his finger down a page, frowning. "I'll put you in with Miss Escuadrille, then. It's room 907, on the top floor but one, just below the dancing." He turned to the hook-covered board behind him and selected a key with a brass tag and handed it to Violet. "Elevators around the corner."

11

Finding Chloe

THE NUMBER ON THE BRASS KEY WAS 907. Violet had never been in an elevator before. It was packed, and it stopped at every floor. A teenage boy in a white uniform worked the controls, and every time they left a floor, Violet's stomach lurched unpleasantly. On the eighth floor, several men got on who reeked of whiskey, a smell Violet recognized from back when Father used to drink it, when alcohol was still legal.

"Goin' down?" one of the men asked tipsily.

"Going up, sir," said the elevator boy.

"Thassallright. We'll go up, then we'll go down." He and his companion laughed uproariously, then tried to sing a song that went, "The red, red, anti-suffrage rose!" These were the only words they could remember, but they managed to sing them three times before the stifling, drunk-smelling elevator reached the ninth floor and Violet tumbled gratefully out.

The corridor was C shaped, and she went around it the wrong way and had to turn and go the other way before she found that room 907 was actually right by the elevator. She turned the key in the door and went in.

The room was tiny but had two iron bedsteads in it. One of them was obviously taken. There was a trunk at the foot of it and a selection of shirtwaists laid out on it, as if the owner had had trouble making up her mind which to wear. There was a straw hat decorated with artificial red roses hanging from a peg, and a clothesline strung across the room held several pairs of black nankeen bloomers, two petticoats, and a corset.

Violet ducked under all of these and sat down on the other bed. The room was sweltering hot, as if all the heat in Nashville had risen up and settled in it. The window was open, and so was the transom over the door. There was an electric fan standing near the window. Violet went over and turned it on.

The underclothes flapped on the clothesline. A stack of papers on the nightstand between the two beds fluttered to the floor, and Violet bent wearily to pick them up. They looked like pamphlets. The top one said on the front, *Men of the South! Now is the time to show your gallantry! Southern women require your aid as never before!*

Violet put the papers back on the nightstand and

weighted them down with an electric curling iron. She flopped back on the bed, feeling hopeless. It was horribly hot in here. It was too hot to move, let alone to go looking for Chloe or to find out what had happened to Mr. Martin and Myrtle. She would have liked to have taken off her clothes, but there was this unknown woman—she of the nankeen bloomers—who was going to come in sooner or later, so Violet couldn't. There was a little door in one corner of the room. Violet went to it. It was a bathroom—well, there was no bathtub, but there was a toilet and a sink. Violet had stayed in hotels twice before, when she'd gone to Scranton with her mother, but she'd never been in a hotel room that had its own toilet. She turned the sink on and splashed water on her face. The water was warm, and it didn't run cold when she left the tap on. But when she wet her hair and neck and stood in front of the fan, she felt a little better.

She was hungry. She got up and went out of the room. She went back to the elevator and pushed the call button. She waited. It was stiflingly hot in the hall. Through the elevator shafts she heard shouts and laughter but no sound of elevators moving. She looked around for the stairs.

It was even hotter in the stairwell. By the time she got down to the eighth floor, Violet couldn't stand the heat anymore. She went out into the hallway, which stank sourly of whiskey. The corridor was full of people, mostly men. They reeled and rolled as if they were standing on the deck of a ship. Some of them were tipsy, but most of them were positively drunk.

A man lurched toward her. His stiff celluloid collar had come loose from all but one of the buttons that held it to his shirt. The collar stood on end on his shoulder, forming a big white C that ended in his right ear. "Here's another Anti, Jim!" he said. "Ask her if there's any more whicks . . . whickskey coming!"

Violet fled back into the stairwell. Halfway down she passed some women wearing yellow roses, and they edged away from her. "Look at that, Anne!" one of them said to the other. "They're using children now. They have no shame at all."

She had forty-two cents in her pocket. She came out into the crowded grand lobby. She could smell food from somewhere. She went down the wide marble steps that led to the main entrance. There was another wide stone staircase leading down to the cellar, and that was where the food smell was coming from. She started down the steps.

"I'm sorry, miss." A man in a white uniform blocked her way. "The Grill Room is for men only."

Violet stared up at him in disbelief. It was one thing to have to use a separate entrance. But she was hungry!

"I have money," she said.

"It's not a matter of money, miss," the man replied, shaking his head. "The Grill Room is for gentlemen. If you go to the dining room on the main floor, they can accommodate you there." He looked at Violet's plaid dress with the double row of gigantic black buttons and the appalling three-inch-wide patent leather belt. "Provided you're suitably attired, of course."

Violet climbed wearily up the stone steps again. She wove her way through the crowd and up a few more steps to the grand dining room. Inside, a brass band was playing, booming through the clink of cutlery on china and the sound of voices. A man in a white tuxedo stood at the entrance. "I'm sorry, miss." He barred her way. "Evening wear is required in the dining room."

Violet didn't have any evening wear. What was the matter with the world that you couldn't even get something to eat when you had forty-two cents in your pocket? She went back up to the front desk.

The desk clerk was counting his tally marks again. He looked up at Violet. "I have a dollar riding on your side," he confided. "Ordinarily I'm not a betting man, but I think you Antis are going to pull this off, I really do."

Violet put her hand to the rose she was wearing. She had forgotten all about it. It had wilted with the heat, and a few petals came off. She looked at them, little bits of velvety crimson in the palm of her hand. She remembered the line the drunks in the elevator had been singing—"The red, red anti-suffrage rose"—and the man who had said, "Here's another Anti!" She'd been too upset to think about it before, but now she realized she'd been taken in by the anti-suffragists. That woman who'd grabbed her at the train station, Charlotte Rowe, was an Anti, and she'd slapped an Anti rose on Violet and taken her up and put her in an Anti room. This was no way to find Chloe!

But first things first. "Where can I get something to eat?" she asked the desk clerk. "They won't let me into the Grill Room downstairs or the dining room."

The desk clerk frowned. "Well, you have to change for dinner, miss. Of course."

"I don't have anything to change into," Violet said. Her other dress wouldn't do either. She was starting to feel very cranky. "Is there anywhere I can just buy something to eat?" She thought about the businesses they had passed on the way from the train station, all closed except the theaters.

"Not at this time of night. Not anyplace that a young lady ought to go into. You'll have to wait till morning."

Violet felt like crying. She didn't care about where a young lady ought to go; she just wanted something to eat. "I can't wait till morning. I'm hungry right now!"

"Hmm." The desk clerk frowned, thinking. "Don't they serve refreshments at your meetings? There should be one going on right now." He nodded upward. "Up there on the mezzanine floor. The Antis' strategy meeting should have sandwiches. I saw the waiters taking them up."

Violet thanked him hurriedly and ran up the narrow stone stairway.

The mezzanine was a broad balcony above the lobby, with a large room set off it by French windows. In the room were many women and a few men, all well dressed, all wearing red roses. Violet didn't really pay much attention to them, though. In the room there was also a stand holding a tray, and on the tray were sandwiches: cucumber sandwiches, sliced cold chicken sandwiches, and cold tongue sandwiches. Violet gathered as many of them as would fit onto one of the little china plates provided. Then she sat down on a chair near the wall and ate.

Nobody in the meeting seemed to have noticed that she had come in. They were all listening to a tall, thin, horse-faced woman in an enormous hat decorated with a flood of red roses and two ghastly green bird wings. She wore three red roses in a row on her lapel.

"I think we can count on Speaker Seth Walker from here on in," the horse-faced woman was saying. "He no longer hearkens to the cry of the suffrage siren. We've got him listening to something else."

A man in the room took two gold coins out of his pocket and jingled them loudly. The people in the room chuckled. Violet ate a cucumber sandwich.

"That's one thing we don't have to worry about, Miss Pearson," a woman in a full-length black bombazine gown said to the horse-faced woman. "Money."

"No, thank goodness," said Miss Pearson. "There are so many gallant men willing to do their utmost to protect the rights of Southern womanhood."

"And an employer's right to hire anybody he wants, including needy children who have dependent parents," the man who had jingled the coins said righteously.

"And, God willing, the rights of the whiskey distillers

to conduct their business freely again someday," said a woman sitting near Violet, but not loud enough to be generally heard.

"So I don't think we need to worry about all that yellow bunting hanging in the capitol," said Miss Pearson. "The Suffs can hang all the yellow bunting they want. Yellow bunting doesn't vote. And neither do they."

People chuckled.

"But what about our resolution to table?" a little woman in a lavender dress squeaked. "It failed."

"It doesn't matter, Miss Claiborne," said Miss Pearson. "We can make as many motions to table as we want. We'll make another tomorrow."

"And besides," said a woman in a floppy straw hat. "There's another little surprise in store for the Suffs tomorrow."

"Now, now, Mrs. Pinckard. Tomorrow evening, of course, is the public meeting at the capitol to discuss the passing of the Susan B. Anthony Amendment." Miss Pearson said the name as though Susan B. Anthony were a woman of particularly evil repute, and several people in the room hissed.

"Passing of it indeed!"

"That's not going to happen."

"Not if we have anything to say about it."

"That's the spirit," said a man near the back of the room. Everybody turned to look at him. "And speaking of spirits, we've just run out in the hospitality room. Not to worry"—he raised a hand—"there's plenty of gold in the kitty, as you all know. We have more coming in from the mountains, but meantime we have sent to Hell's Half-Acre for a small supply to tide us over."

The Antis were bribing people! Violet thought. They'd bribed that Seth Walker fella to make him change sides. And they were serving illegal alcohol to legislators up on the eighth floor—that's why those drunks were up there.

"Bootleg stuff from Hell's Half-Acre will make you blind," another man observed.

"Then we'll lead the legislators up to the capitol by the hand and help them cast their votes."

Miss Pearson gestured for silence. "We're ahead of the game. The Suffs were counting on Walker, and losing him to us was a serious setback for them. We're going to win this. . . ."

There were mutters of "yes!" and "hear, hear!"

"But not without a fight. Tomorrow, we need all hands at the capitol."

Violet combined a cucumber and a chicken sandwich and ate them together as an experiment.

"Governor Roberts is not on our side. He's made no secret of the fact that he's a Suff. We need to ride herd on all our men and do whatever it takes to keep them loyal. And if need be, we may have to be prepared to remove a few of the Suffs' men from the picture."

Violet had finished her sandwiches, and she got up to

get a few more. Everyone was listening with rapt attention to Miss Pearson and nobody seemed to care how many sandwiches Violet was taking. They had probably already eaten in the dining room. *They* were suitably attired. Hanging on the wall behind Miss Pearson was the flag of the Confederate States of America. Violet recognized it from her history books at school. But the Civil War had been over for fifty-five years. What was the matter with these people? Didn't they even know what country they lived in?

Why were all these women against woman suffrage anyway? Violet could understand how a woman could just never have thought one way or another about voting but not how a woman could be *against* it. Well, except Mother was.

Violet drifted out of the room to the balcony and stood looking down at the lobby below. The railing was low—too low to lean on—so she didn't stand too close. She stood beside a garland of plaster fruit that decorated an arch in the ceiling and chewed a cold tongue sandwich thoughtfully. From up here, you could actually hear what people were saying.

A balding, stoop-shouldered man in a brown suit stood below her. He was wearing a yellow rose in his lapel and talking to a woman in a white dress with a yellow sash.

"It's a shame about Seth Walker, Miss Pollitzer," he said. "That's a blow. How many do we have now?"

"I'm not sure, Mr. Hanover," the lady in white said. "Miss Mayhew is working on the latest numbers now."

Violet almost dropped her tongue sandwich when she heard the name Mayhew.

"Oh, here she comes now."

This time Violet did drop her sandwich, and it fell over the railing. Violet didn't stop to see where it hit. She put her plate down on the floor and turned and clattered down the stone staircase, having the presence of mind to drop her red rose on the stairs as she went.

She might not have recognized the woman coming toward her if she hadn't heard those people say "Mayhew." Chloe was wearing a smart sky blue walking suit and a straw hat with a yellow rose in it. Looking under the hat, Violet could see that Chloe had bobbed her brown hair—it only just reached her collar. Mother would have had a fit. There were shadows under Chloe's dark brown eyes that made her look older than her twenty-three years.

"Hello, Chloe," Violet said.

Chloe stared at Violet as if she were a giraffe. "Violet! What on earth?" Then she ran forward and threw her arms around Violet.

Violet hugged Chloe, embarrassed. Theirs was not a hugging family. They let go of each other quickly.

"Violet, what on earth, how on earth . . ." She took a step back and looked nervous. "Violet, Mother and Father aren't here, are they?"

"No," said Violet. "I, um . . ." To say she had run away suddenly seemed melodramatic in the face of sensible Chloe in her sensible suit. "I kind of left." She felt a need to justify herself, so she added, "They never gave me any of your letters. And then I found them in Mother's desk when I was looking for a stamp."

"Oh, Violet! Then what happened?"

Mr. Hanover and Miss Pollitzer listened politely.

"I just got mad and left," said Violet. "And then I went to New York, and . . . well, anyway, here I am."

"I can't believe you came all this way alone!"

"I wasn't exactly alone," said Violet. She wasn't sure how to explain about Mr. Martin and Myrtle, particularly now that she had lost them.

Chloe turned to the other two. "I beg your pardon. This is my sister, Violet. Violet, this is Miss Anita Pollitzer of the National Woman's Party and Mr. Joe Hanover, a representative from Memphis who's leading the suffrage fight in the House."

Violet turned and curtsied carefully. "How do you do," she said politely. "I'm very pleased to meet you."

"Likewise, I'm sure," said Miss Pollitzer.

"How do you do," said Mr. Hanover politely.

"Chloe, you'd better go get this taken care of," said Miss Pollitzer, nodding at Violet. "But did you get those numbers?"

"I think so." Chloe handed Miss Pollitzer a piece of paper. "If they're uncommitted, I put a question mark next to them, and if they might change sides, I put two question marks. I might not make it to the meeting tonight. Excuse us."

Violet curtsied again and then followed Chloe briskly across the lobby toward the women's entrance.

The Tulane Hotel, where Chloe and the other National Woman's Party members were staying, was two blocks away, downhill, and Violet noticed when they got outside that it hadn't gotten any cooler even though it was fully dark now. The Tulane was only six stories high instead of ten, and it was less intimidating than the Hermitage.

There was a long line of cars parked out front, and Chloe and Violet stopped to visit the Hope Chest.

Henry Ford had said, famously, that you could have any color Model T you wanted as long as it was black, but you actually could get other colors. The Hope Chest was dark green, with black fenders and running boards and a black collapsible roof. It was a runabout, with a leather front seat big enough to hold a driver and a passenger but no backseat. Instead, there was an open space behind the cab, which had been fitted with a small wooden truck bed. "For carrying stuff," Chloe explained.

They admired the car's pressed steel radiator, its nickel hubcaps and narrow, wire-spoked wheels, the nickel radiator cap, and the big round electric headlamps, which Violet said looked like bug eyes.

"Like frog eyes," said Chloe fondly. "And it's amphibious too, the Hope Chest is, like a frog. I've driven it right through streams, especially this last month, when I've been up in the mountains, hunting down Tennessee legislators in their dens."

She patted the Hope Chest on its steel hood. "It's my freedom, the Hope Chest. And women have been using automobiles so much this last year, they might really give us freedom. I mean freedom to be real, voting citizens of the United States." She sighed. "If there's time, I'll teach you to drive it."

The Tulane lobby was just as big as that of the Hermitage but less grand, with wooden pillars and paneling and marble floors (there seemed to be a lot of marble in Nashville, Violet thought). There were no crowds—just a few people here and there in armchairs reading the evening paper and a few women wearing yellow sashes or yellow roses passing through.

On the way inside, Violet finished her explanation of how she'd gotten to Nashville, which she'd started as they walked from the Hermitage.

"And you wired Mother and Father from Washington and let them know you were all right?" Chloe asked.

"Yes. Mr. Martin made me," Violet said.

"Good. I'm sure they must be frantic." Chloe got her key from the desk clerk, who was playing pinochle with a drummer (as traveling salesmen were called). The drummer had his hat on.

Violet thought it was odd of Chloe to take Mother and Father's side, considering Chloe wasn't on speaking terms with either of them. "I don't think they're frantic. But anyway, I told them I was all right. Mr. Martin paid for it."

"Well, I think you should write them again. I'm not sure how long we're going to be here, but they'll be worried," said Chloe as they climbed the stairs to the second floor.

It seemed like no matter how many times she mentioned Mr. Martin's name, Chloe wasn't going to say anything about him. If Mr. Martin was sweet on Chloe, Violet thought, it must be one-sided. Violet was more concerned about "how long we're going to be here." Chloe didn't seem as happy as she should have been to see Violet.

"But I'm going to stay with you," Violet said. "Maybe you should be the one to write and tell them that. They don't listen to me."

"We'll see," said Chloe.

"Aren't you worried about Mr. Martin?" said Violet, trying again. "Those agents that were after him?"

"No," said Chloe firmly, turning the key in the lock and opening the door. "Oh, don't look at me like that, Violet! This ax has been hanging over Theo's—over Mr. Martin's head all the time I've known him, and I can't worry about it anymore."

Violet thought that was unkind, but Chloe looked so exhausted that Violet decided not to say anything. She looked around the room. It had two iron bedsteads, like the room in the Hermitage, but it was a bit bigger. Both beds were clearly taken, which Violet guessed meant she would have to share with Chloe.

"I'm sorry, I know that sounds mean," said Chloe. "But you know, Violet, you can't change people. Most of us find that out the hard way—I'm telling you for free. Do you want some Chero-Cola?"

There was a rattle of ice in a bucket, and the pop of a bottle opener, and Chloe handed Violet a soft drink bottle.

"Thanks," Violet said, and took a long gulp of the Chero-Cola. It was very sweet, and she instantly felt less tired. She tried to pass the bottle back to Chloe.

"No, you go ahead and finish it," said Chloe, sitting down on the bed with a sigh and taking off her shoes. "Don't worry about Mr. Martin, Violet. He can take care of himself."

"What about Myrtle?" Violet demanded.

"He can take care of her too," said Chloe, unlooping her stockings from her garters.

"What if he gets arrested? What's going to happen to Myrtle then?" Violet was getting frustrated. She had been counting on Chloe to take charge and fix things, not to take off her shoes and look exhausted.

Chloe frowned. "I don't know. You're right, Violet. I don't know."

She stood up and left the room abruptly, and Violet heard her padding down the hall. To the bathroom, Violet assumed.

Violet stooped down and unlaced her own shoes. It was hot in here too, and the open window and transom that were supposed to catch a breeze didn't, because there wasn't one to catch. There was a fan on the windowsill, but when Violet went over to turn it on, she saw that it took nickels. She wasn't sure if it was worth it to spend any of her small store of cash for a few minutes of breeze. It looked like Chloe intended to go to sleep now. Violet would probably be expected to go to sleep too, even though she didn't know what had become of Myrtle. It was very frustrating.

The door creaked open. "I'm sorry, Violet. I'm just so tired. I don't know what we can do about your friend. We could call the police, but—"

"No," said Violet, alarmed. "If Mr. Martin hasn't been caught, we don't want to call the police!"

"Right," said Chloe. "I'm not sure if they'd even bother to look for a lost colored girl anyway, or what they'd do with her when they found her. Oh, dear. And you don't even know what town they left the train in?"

Violet shook her head. "I just know it was about an hour after we left Chattanooga."

"Well, I guess the first thing is to find out which town it was," said Chloe. "If we have to, we can drive over there in the Hope Chest." She sighed. "Tomorrow, why don't you go over to the train station and look at the timetable and see if you can't figure out which town it was."

"Okay," said Violet.

Chloe flopped down on the bed with a creak of springs. "How is Stephen?" she said.

Violet was busy thinking about Myrtle and Mr. Martin, and it took her a second to remember who Stephen was—their brother, of course. "He's the same as ever."

"Oh, dear," said Chloe tiredly. "And Mother? How is Mother?"

"The same as ever," said Violet shortly.

"I really am glad you're here, Violet." Chloe put an arm up to cover her eyes. "I'm just so tired. And I have a lot of other things on my mind right now. Don't forget to brush your teeth before you go to bed."

And she fell asleep before Violet could point out that she'd left her toothbrush at the Hermitage.

12

Violet Spies

VIOLET SPENT A HOT, MISERABLE NIGHT sharing a bed with Chloe and thinking that it would have been cooler in the Hermitage, where you didn't have to pay for the fan. But in the morning Violet had an idea.

She woke up stiffly next to Chloe, who was still asleep. A young woman was walking around the room, eating a bowl of Grape-Nuts. Violet figured this woman must be Miss Lewis, who Chloe had told her was the lady who had the other bed.

Violet dressed hurriedly and wanted to run out to the train station to start looking for Myrtle, but Miss Lewis insisted she should eat some Grape-Nuts first. They were supposed to be very good for you. There wasn't a spoon or any milk, so Violet scooped them up from the bowl with her fingers and chewed while Miss Lewis talked.

"Today's the fourth day the legislature has met," Miss Lewis said. "We were hoping it would all be over by now. The first day they tried to pass a joint resolution in the Tennessee House and Senate, and we thought we had enough votes, but the Antis had bribed a lot of the men we were counting on." She wiped a hand over her forehead, which was already sweating.

"How long will they meet for?" Violet asked.

"We don't know," said Miss Lewis. "The Senate and House have to vote separately now, and they each have to pass the amendment. And we don't know when they will. The Antis are trying to bribe as many legislators as they can, and they won't let the vote happen now until they're sure they can win."

"Aren't the Suffs bribing legislators?" said Violet. She was too tired to think straight, or she would have realized how rude this sounded.

"Certainly not!" said Miss Lewis. "Women are entering politics to clean it up, not to add to the filth!

"When women vote, there will be no more bribery or corruption. There will be no more war. The concerns of mothers will become the concerns of the government—good schools, safe food, and temperance. Just think, the United States has banned alcohol completely, and soon temperance will spread to other nations, so that nowhere on earth will mankind ever be a slave to alcohol again!"

Violet had finished her Grape-Nuts. "Excuse me, Miss Lewis," she said. "I need to go to the train station."

"I'm sure those Antis are going to use every dirty trick they can think of to block the legislature," said Miss Lewis, seeming not to hear her. "If only there was some way we could know what they're planning!"

As she walked along, Violet reflected that she had sat in an Anti meeting last night, eating sandwiches, and that nobody had even noticed she was there.

She was perfectly set up, Violet thought, to be a spy. She could go back to the Hermitage, pretend to be an Anti, and tell the Suffs what the Antis were planning. She wanted to do something to help—since meeting that hatchet-faced woman in Chattanooga yesterday, she found she cared about woman suffrage very much. It was more than just a newspaper story to her now.

Violet looked at the rail yards that she was walking past. She saw two hoboes walking along, carrying small bundles under their arms. They looked like they had just gotten off a train, and they reminded Violet of Hobie the Hobo. She wondered if he'd gotten to Florida yet.

The smaller hobo let out a cry and grabbed the bigger hobo's arm, pointing to Violet.

Violet started. Hoboes could be dangerous; she'd gathered that much from Hobie, who had been careful not to let her and Myrtle meet any other hoboes. She turned to run.

"Violet!" called the larger hobo, and relief washed over Violet. She ran toward them, the gravel roadbed crunching under her feet.

"I was just on my way to look for you," she said.

"We shook those Palmer agents," said Myrtle. "They're running around the Tennessee backwoods looking for us." She pointed back down the rails, toward the freight yard. "We rode in a caboose!"

"But . . ." Violet looked at Myrtle and then at Mr. Martin. They were both rather soot-covered, though not as much as Violet and Myrtle had been after riding in the blind behind the engine with Hobie. "Mr. Martin, you jumped off the train. I saw you."

Mr. Martin shrugged and smiled. "Sorry to scare you, Violet. I had to make it look like I jumped so that agent would leave us all alone. I went over onto the steps of the vestibule of the connecting car, then climbed up onto the roof and rode there till the next stop. Then I got into a different car."

"And you told *us* it was dangerous to ride freight trains!" Violet said.

Mr. Martin shrugged again. "Well, it is. Have you, um, found your sister yet, Violet?"

"Yes," said Violet. "She's at the Tulane Hotel; it's just up the hill here. She'll be so glad to see you."

Violet wasn't sure if this was true, but it was the sort of polite thing she'd always been taught to say.

Chloe was just coming down the stairs into the big wood-paneled lobby of the Tulane, wearing her sky blue walking suit and the straw hat with a yellow rose in it. She still looked exhausted, Violet thought. She looked like she hadn't slept at all.

Chloe got to the bottom of the stairs and stopped, looking at Mr. Martin for a moment as if she wasn't sure who he was. She didn't notice Violet and Myrtle at all. Violet watched Chloe and Mr. Martin look at each other. The desk clerk and the drummer he was playing cards with watched too. Chloe's mouth opened a little bit and she froze. Mr. Martin turned faintly pink under the train soot, and Violet could almost hear him wishing he'd stopped to wash his face.

Chloe's face turned pink too. "Theo, what were you thinking, helping my sister run away from home?"

"He didn't help me run away from home; I did it by myself," Violet said, annoyed.

Chloe spared Violet a glance and then looked back at Mr. Martin again.

"I'm delighted to see you too," said Mr. Martin sarcastically.

"Theo, you shouldn't have left New York." Chloe spoke very quietly, and Violet guessed she was trying not to let the desk clerk and drummer overhear.

"I wasn't aware I needed your permission to leave New York," Mr. Martin said.

"Theo, stop it. What happened? Did the federal agents find the safe house?"

"No. Your sister came crashing in on me."

Violet felt she had by no means come crashing in, but

the way the two of them were glaring at each other now, she didn't really want to be involved in their discussion.

"Why didn't you send her home, Theo?"

"Because it's impossible to make you headstrong Mayhew women do anything you don't want to," said Mr. Martin testily.

"I see you're still thinking in terms of *making* women do things," Chloe snapped.

"That's completely unfair, and you know it!" Mr. Martin said.

Violet and Myrtle exchanged glances. Unfortunately, this was enough to draw attention to Myrtle.

"Hey!" the desk clerk barked, and everyone turned to look at him. "Uh-uh. We don't allow *them* in here." He pointed.

They all stared at him.

"You mean Myrtle?" Mr. Martin said in a dangerously gentle voice. He stepped over and put a hand on Myrtle's shoulder.

"If you don't mind, we're trying to have a conversation here," said Chloe to the desk clerk.

"Have it somewhere else, then," said the desk clerk. "Not in my hotel."

"I *happen* to be a guest here," said Chloe. She put her hand on Myrtle's other shoulder.

"Not if you're going to bring in coloreds and parade them around the lobby," the desk clerk snarled.

"Yeah, this is a high-tone establishment," said the

drummer, shuffling the cards and pushing his hat back on his head.

"Have you two eaten?" Chloe asked Mr. Martin.

"No, we were just going to look for something. . . ."

"Do you need any money? I mean, to get the child something to eat," Chloe said. Violet noticed that they were both looking at Myrtle now and that neither of them seemed angry anymore.

"No, thanks, I have—"

"Are you going to get that colored kid out of here or am I going to have to call somebody?" the desk clerk asked.

"We're leaving," said Mr. Martin. "I'm sure we can find someplace where they'll take our kind in. Even in Nashville," he added, giving the desk clerk a nasty look.

"Can't imagine where," said the desk clerk. "There's colored hotels, of course, but you ain't colored."

"I don't think I like Nashville," Myrtle said to Violet when they got out to the street.

"I'm not so sure I like it either," said Mr. Martin, overhearing her.

"Well, it's your own . . . ," Chloe started to retort, but then seemed to think better of it. "Nashville is where it's all come down to, Theo. We're going to win or lose everything in Nashville. And I'm staying right here until we do."

Mr. Martin went over to the curb. "How's the old Hope Chest holding up?"

Chloe followed him. "Pretty well. I replaced the brass radiator with one of those steel ones, like you suggested."

"Excellent." Mr. Martin stroked the radiator. "And I was right, wasn't I?"

"Yes," said Chloe fondly. "It hardly ever overheats now."

Violet noticed that Chloe seemed suddenly happier and much less tired than she'd been a few minutes ago.

Myrtle noticed too. "I don't think your sister's going to send Mr. Martin to the rightabout," she murmured.

"No, it's the car she's sweet on, not him," Violet said.

"Uh-huh," said Myrtle skeptically.

"We should drive her out into the country, take a picnic," said Mr. Martin. "There are some beautiful places east of Nashville."

"And I could teach the girls to drive," Chloe said.

At the words "the girls," Mr. Martin turned around and looked at Violet and Myrtle. He had clearly forgotten they were there.

"Let me go get this one something to eat," he said. "And find a place to park her. There has to be a hotel that takes white and colored in this town somewhere."

Violet watched them go with regret. She hadn't realized it until now, but she hadn't seen a single colored person at the Hermitage or the Tulane. She was sorry that Myrtle wasn't going to be able to stay with her.

Maybe when women got the vote, they'd be able to change that.

13

Dead Horse Alley

MR. MARTIN WAS WRONG—THERE WAS NOT one hotel in Nashville that would take in a white man and a colored child. Myrtle realized this a lot sooner than Mr. Martin did. She tried to tell him, but he just got more and more irritable and wouldn't listen. They couldn't even find anywhere to eat lunch.

At the first drugstore, they went in and sat down at the lunch counter. The boy at the counter didn't even speak to them. He simply called to the druggist in the back to telephone the police. Myrtle didn't have much trouble getting Mr. Martin out of there. At the next place, the boy behind the counter told them that if they went around to the alley door, he could serve them. Or, he added generously, Mr. Martin could eat at the lunch counter and Myrtle could eat in the alley.

"Or I can take my business elsewhere," Mr. Martin snapped.

"Why don't you take it back up north?" said the boy. "If you don't want to respect our Southern customs."

After the fourth drugstore, Myrtle suggested that they eat in the alley because she was getting hungry. So that's what they did, sitting on stone steps behind a drugstore beside an overflowing garbage can, eating egg salad sandwiches and sipping chocolate phosphates.

"At least prices are cheap in the South," said Mr. Martin, who had paid twenty cents for their lunch.

"I don't think I like it here," Myrtle repeated.

Myrtle's people had lived in Washington ever since the Civil War. Washington wasn't exactly the South, her mother had always said, but it wasn't exactly the North either. Mama had sometimes talked about moving to the North. She would have been happy that Myrtle ended up in New York. But Myrtle didn't care for the Girls' Training Institute, and she knew Mama wouldn't have cared for it either. Mama had meant for Myrtle to get an education and do something in the world. Something besides be somebody's maid.

Mr. Martin seemed to get the point about the hotels quicker, perhaps because of their experience at the Tulane. Most of the hotels probably didn't have room anyway, Myrtle thought, because the entire city seemed to be full of visitors wearing yellow or red roses. But the hotels with doormen stopped them at the door, and in those without, the desk clerks shook their heads and said, "Uh-uh."

"They have to take us in one of these places," Mr. Martin said as they crossed Capitol Hill and came down on the other side to a row of disreputable-looking hotels and rooming houses, which seemed to be leaning on each other for support. They went into one that said *Rooms Twenty-five Cents* over the door.

They walked into a gloomy lobby furnished with weak-backed chairs and a grease-stained sofa that looked like it had fought in the Civil War and lost. Men who seemed to be as much a part of the decor as the tobacco-stained carpet were slumped on the furniture, looking as if they had become one with it.

The clerk at the desk sat behind a protective brass cage—in case any of the men in the lobby came to life and attacked, Myrtle supposed. He seemed less affronted than the clerks in the other hotels at the idea that he might have room for Myrtle.

"Sorry, we don't take colored," he said. "We try to run a nice hotel here."

Myrtle looked around at the men on the chairs, one of whom was swigging enthusiastically out of a brown bottle labeled *Best Stomach Bitters*. A cloud of cigarette smoke hovered between their heads and the ceiling. Cigarette butts were scattered around the men's feet.

"To tell the truth, sir," said the desk clerk, "we don't allow ladies here anyways. Not even white ones. You can never tell with females, sir, and we do try to keep the place decent."

"I can see that," said Mr. Martin. "Tell me, is it too much to hope that there's anywhere we can lodge in this great city of Nashville?"

"Well, there's a woman down in Crappy Chute that takes in colored," said the desk clerk, thinking. "No, come to think of it, I guess she was burned out in the 1916 fire. Now, there's a colored YMCA downtown, but of course they won't take the child. Or you either, come to think of it. Now, if you want to send her over to Hell's Half-Acre . . ."

"I'm not sending a seven-year-old girl to a place called Hell's Half-Acre," Mr. Martin said.

"I'm ten, sir," Myrtle reminded him.

"Oh, that's just the name." The desk clerk shrugged. "Smoky Roll's just as bad. Here." He dipped his pen in ink and wrote a name and address on a piece of paper. "This woman on Dead Horse Alley rents to colored people. Just head on up Sixth Avenue, cross the Louisville and Nashville tracks, and . . . and then ask someone else for directions."

Mr. Martin took the paper. "Thanks."

The desk clerk leaned forward against the brass bars of his cage. "Listen, young man," he said, dropping his voice so that Myrtle had to strain to hear him. "I know what it looks like to you Northerners, the way we do things in the South. Our special customs. But we have a very harmonious relationship between the races down here. Very harmonious."

Mr. Martin opened his mouth to answer this, but Myrtle grabbed his arm and led him quickly to the door.

They walked up Sixth Avenue away from the capitol. The street was cobbled with gray brick-shaped stones and had concrete sidewalks that sloped and slouched disconsolately into the street. Two-story brick buildings lined the street, with wooden water towers rising above them here and there.

An advertisement painted on the side of a brick building showed two colored children of indeterminate sex, both wearing full skirts and nothing else. They had round white eyes and bright red lips. Between them was a sink full of soapsuds, and they were both holding up freshly scrubbed dishes that shone like diamonds—painted rays surrounding the dishes to show how much they were shining. More glowing dishes hung behind them. Beside one child was a box of Gold Dust cleansing powder. Underneath them were painted the words *Your Servants, Ma'am!*

The sign reminded Myrtle of the Girls' Training Institute, and she felt instantly depressed. "I don't want to ever be anybody's servant," she said.

"I agree," said Mr. Martin. "Don't be. Excuse me, sir."

The colored man Mr. Martin called to looked surprised at being called sir. He touched his hat deferentially and gave Mr. Martin directions to the address the desk clerk had written down. Mr. Martin touched his own hat in return. Myrtle thought the two men were making each other very uncomfortable.

It got worse when they got to Dead Horse Alley. They had run out of brick houses and stone streets by then. There was a smell of outhouses and rotting food on the hot air, and foul water ran down a gutter at the side of the street. The houses were made of wood, mostly unpainted or painted so long ago that you could no longer tell what color they were supposed to be.

"I guess this must be Dead Horse Alley," said Mr. Martin. "According to those directions that fella gave me." He sounded doubtful. Myrtle could see why. It didn't look like an alley. It looked like a dry gully cut by a rushing creek that would be back again the next time it rained. It wasn't even flat. There was no way you could have driven a wagon up it, even if it had been wide enough.

A woman was sitting on the stoop of what looked like a cowshed, sewing. "Yes, this is Dead Horse Alley," she said.

"Can you tell us where we might find Mrs. Eugenia Ready, ma'am?" Mr. Martin asked.

"I'm Mrs. Eugenia Ready," said the woman. She stood up. She was older than Mama would've been, Myrtle thought, but not really old. She wore an old-fashioned blue dress that came to her ankles and had her hair done up on top of her head but not straightened. Mama had never straightened her hair either. But this woman was looking at them both a little suspiciously, and she got more suspicious when Mr. Martin explained that they were looking for lodgings.

The problem, it seemed, was that Mr. Martin wanted to stay there too. Mrs. Ready was uncomfortable with that. She seemed to be thinking that if Mr. Martin wanted to stay in a place like Dead Horse Alley, he must be on the run from the law or something. Mr. Martin's evil-looking scar probably encouraged her impression, which, Myrtle had to admit, was correct. She quoted a high price, two dollars a week, but Mr. Martin accepted it without demurral and she seemed to feel she had no choice but to let them inside.

The house really had been a cowshed at one point; Myrtle was sure of it. A wooden floor had been put down, and the place was scrupulously clean, but it still smelled faintly of cows. The two partitioned-off bedrooms reminded Myrtle of stalls. One of them was clearly Mrs. Ready's room. The other one she supposed Mr. Martin would get, and she'd have to be in the kitchen. The kitchen had a wood cookstove, a dry sink, and a table covered with a checkered oilcloth. A treadle sewing machine stood against the wall. There was a shelf with a Bible on it and a wedding picture of Mrs. Ready and some fellow who must be Mr. Ready. Next to it was a picture of a serious-looking young colored lady with round glasses. Next to that was a yellow rose stuck in a bottle.

"The girl is my daughter, Rosalie. She's in preparatory classes for Fisk University. She aims to be a doctor. There's a colored medical school, Meharry, in Nashville," said Mrs. Ready. "The gentleman is my husband, Walter. He was killed in the Dutch Bend train derailment in 1918."

"I'm sorry, ma'am," said Myrtle.

Mr. Martin looked like he was thinking of saying something Bolshevist about railroads and thought better of it. Myrtle had learned on their travels that he thought railroads were all run by robber barons who didn't care if their workers and passengers died. "I'm sorry to hear it, ma'am. Does that yellow rose mean . . ."

"Yes, I'm a suffragist," said Mrs. Ready defiantly. "And I support the Susan B. Anthony Amendment."

"So do we," said Myrtle.

"Well, just stay out of sight, child," said Mrs. Ready. "That's our job this week." She sounded bitter.

"I can always stay out of sight, ma'am," said Myrtle. "I can turn invisible."

"Child, we can all do that," said Mrs. Ready.

Chloe had thought Violet's idea of being a spy was an excellent one. "And you can report to me several times a day," she said. "You can come down to the Tulane, or I'll go up to the Hermitage."

"No, that won't work," said Violet. "Everyone knows the Tulane's a Suff base, so I can't go in there with my red rose on, and I can't be seen talking to Suffs at the Hermitage."

They'd agreed to meet instead at Max Bloomstein's Pharmacy for lunch at noon each day, neither of them wearing Suff or Anti symbols. Violet thought it sounded exciting and spylike. Like something from the movies.

Going back to the Hermitage was less exciting. The ninth floor of the Hermitage was somehow hotter than she remembered. When she turned the key and opened the door to room 907, she saw that the clothesline full of nankeen bloomers had been taken down and their occupant was in possession of the room.

"Oh!" said the woman, startled.

"I beg your pardon," said Violet. "I'm Miss Violet Mayhew; they, um, gave me that other bed."

"Oh!" The woman's mouth was shaped like an O, so maybe it was the easiest sound for her to make. She was stout, and not much taller than Violet, and about thirty years old. She had brass-colored hair, piled up under a spreading pink hat, and round, startled blue eyes. She was wearing a flouncy pink dress that Violet would have considered too babyish for herself.

"I'm Miss Annasette Escuadrille," she said. "I was just getting ready for the thing tonight." She nodded at the bedside table, and Violet saw that the electric curling iron was now plugged in. How anyone could want more heat on a day like this she couldn't imagine.

Still, she might as well get right to spying. "What thing?" she asked, sitting down on her bed. "I mean, I know there's a thing, but I forgot."

Miss Escuadrille untied the ribbons that held on her hat and began unpinning her hair. "I don't know, some thing at the capitol? Miss Charlotte Rowe is going to speak; have you met her?"

"Yes," said Violet. "I met her at the train station."

"She's so clever," said Miss Escuadrille. "And Miss Josephine Anderson Pearson will be there, and Senator Candler, of course, and Mrs. James S. Pinckard . . . and some Suffs too, I suppose."

"Are they going to vote on the amendment?" said Violet.

"I don't think so," said Miss Escuadrille, opening the metal clamp on the hair curler, rolling a lock of brass-colored hair around it, and snapping the curler shut. "I don't really understand all that part of it. It's just some sort of meeting. There'll be speeches."

A dreadful smell of burned hair filled the room.

"Do you want to use this next?" Miss Escuadrille asked.

"No, thank you," said Violet, who couldn't imagine putting hot metal next to her face in this heat. Besides, her hair wouldn't hold a curl anyway. She wondered if Miss Escuadrille would mind if she turned the fan on.

"I just think we all need to look really nice," said Miss Escuadrille, looking at Violet's plaid dress with the horrible patent leather belt. "Because you know the Suffs are going to look like frumpy man-hating witches."

Violet felt moved to retort that at least the Suffs didn't

wear flouncy pink dresses better suited to a four-year-old, but she remembered that she was supposed to be an Anti and kept her mouth shut.

"I was on duty at the telegraph offices all morning," said Miss Escuadrille. "Every time a Suff goes in to send a message, I go look at the desk after she's sent it and see if I can read the impressions the pen has left on the blotter." She shrugged and reached for another strand of hair. "Then whenever a messenger boy heads out with a telegram, I try to catch him before he gets on his bike to bribe him to show me the message. But I can't catch them." She shrugged again. "They move so fast."

"Would they really show you the telegrams for money?" Violet asked, surprised.

"Supposed to," said Miss Escuadrille. "And then if it's addressed to a Suff and you don't want them to get it, they're supposed to give you the telegram for more money."

Miss Escuadrille was either the stupidest adult Violet had ever met or just didn't know what "supposed to" meant, Violet thought.

"Don't you have another dress you could wear?" said Miss Escuadrille.

Violet unwrapped her bundle and showed Miss Escuadrille the other dress that had been cut down for her in Washington. It was a brown-and-black houndstooth check and looked as if it was meant to subdue whoever wore it into a deep and prolonged state of melancholy.

"Huh," said Miss Escuadrille. "That won't do.

Makes you look like a Suff. Or a Bolshevik. I'll see if we can round up something better. I'm sure Mrs. Pinckard can find something. Or buy it if she has to—we have plenty of money."

"Why do we have plenty of money?" Violet asked. She had been wondering this since the meeting last night.

"Because of the generosity and true chivalry of Southern men," said Miss Escuadrille blithely. "They don't ever want women to have to vote. They know that Southern women were meant to be the queens of their households, so voting would be demeaning to us."

Violet took this to mean that Miss Escuadrille didn't know where the money was coming from. "But Miss Escuadrille, you're not even married," she said. "So how can you be the queen of a household?"

To Violet's dismay, Miss Escuadrille's eyes filled up with tears. "What a horrible, cruel, nasty thing to say to a person!"

She sat down on her bed, which creaked alarmingly, and buried her face in her hands, sobbing.

Violet dived for the curling iron, which had fallen on the rug. She missed the wooden handle and grabbed the business end instead, burning her fingers painfully. She unplugged the curling iron from the wall socket.

"I'm sorry, Miss Escuadrille," she apologized. "I beg your pardon."

"Horrible . . . not my fault . . . not married!" Miss Escuadrille sobbed.

"I'm really, really sorry. I didn't mean it that way."

"How would you like it? To get to be my age and not even married!" Miss Escuadrille was getting more and more out of breath between sobs, and Violet wondered if she might be becoming hysterical. In books, when people got hysterical, you slapped them in the face. Violet didn't think she'd do that.

Instead, she sat back down on her bed and went on apologizing every time Miss Escuadrille stopped sobbing long enough to hear her. In between apologies she sucked her burned fingers. She thought about the hatchet-faced woman in the train station in Chattanooga, waiting for her son's body to arrive from France. She was Southern, that woman, but she hadn't looked like the queen of anything.

This spying was a lot less fun than Violet had thought it would be. She wished Myrtle were there.

14

Max Bloomstein's Pharmacy

MR. MARTIN HADN'T SAID ANYTHING ABOUT how long they were staying in Dead Horse Alley or where they were going afterward. Myrtle supposed that, like everyone else, they were waiting. They had been there for two days already, but Mrs. Ready had told them that no one was sure when the legislature would vote.

Myrtle didn't know what they would do after the legislature voted. She had no plans. She didn't want to go back to the Girls' Training Institute, and she didn't want to stay in Tennessee, but she wasn't really sure what other choices she had. None, it seemed like.

Myrtle would have liked to have gone and found Violet. It would have been fun to go exploring together, but she had seen enough of Tennessee by now to know that was impossible.

Mrs. Ready had gone out to deliver some of the sewing she did for a living and then to visit her daughter. This was a relief. Myrtle felt she could have gotten along fine with Mrs. Ready if it wasn't for Mr. Martin, but Mr. Martin made the whole situation very uncomfortable. Mrs. Ready was always casting suspicious looks at him, trying to figure out what he was hiding from and why he was missing three fingers and why he had Myrtle with him.

Myrtle had been trying to keep Mr. Martin inside and out of sight. He didn't seem to be taking the fact that he was a wanted man very seriously, and Myrtle felt somebody had to. She had gone out for newspapers to keep him busy, and for groceries—sardines and peaches and Uneeda biscuits. But now Mr. Martin seemed determined to go out. He announced that he had to go and talk to people to see if there was any news. Myrtle didn't see any way she could actually forbid him to leave, and she privately suspected which person in particular he wanted to see.

Myrtle could see that the problem of Mr. Martin's future needed to be settled nearly as much as hers did. "Miss Chloe sure is pretty," she commented.

"Uh-huh," said Mr. Martin, crawling under the bed to look for his socks.

"You should tell her that you love her."

There was a loud, metallic clang from under the bed and Mr. Martin emerged, rubbing his head. "Myrtle, that's crazy talk. Be quiet."

"You should get married," Myrtle suggested.

"I'm a fugitive," said Mr. Martin, smiling thinly. "Do you know what a fugitive is, Myrtle?"

"Of course," said Myrtle. "So do your time, and then marry her."

"My 'time' is likely to be twenty years in Fort Leavenworth," said Mr. Martin, tying his shoes with unnecessary vigor. "Unless they deport me, which would be if I was lucky."

Myrtle frowned. Twenty years was a lot. Miss Chloe, being so pretty, was likely to marry someone else in that time. More to the point, Myrtle would be very old in twenty years and wouldn't need a family anymore. "Maybe you should go to China," she said.

"It's a thought," said Mr. Martin. "Myrtle, I'm going out, and I want you to stay here and wait. Can I trust you for that?"

Myrtle ignored the question. "You could take Miss Chloe to China with you," she said. "And then get married. And you might want to have a kid."

"Myrtle, will you stay here and not move?"

"Not a baby, maybe," said Myrtle. "Babies are a lot of trouble. But an older kid, you know."

"Yes, that sounds like an excellent idea. Now stay here, Myrtle, and I'll be back in an hour or so."

"Are you sure you would get twenty years?" said Myrtle. "I knew a fella in D.C. who cut another fella with a razor, and he only got three months."

"Isn't it amazing?" said Mr. Martin, half sarcastically

and half seriously. "But I'm going to get twenty years. Most of my friends did. Big Bill Haywood did. And I will too."

A thought struck Myrtle that had not previously occurred to her. Maybe Mr. Martin had actually done something really serious.

Maybe he had killed somebody.

"Mr. Martin, why are those agents chasing you?" Myrtle asked.

Mr. Martin frowned and straightened his soft collar in the mirror that hung on the wall. "Back in 1918, I spoke out against the War."

"Spoke out against it?" Myrtle said.

"Yes. I said we shouldn't have been in it—that it wasn't our war."

Myrtle stared. "That's it? That's what they're after you for?"

"What, you don't think that's enough?" Again Myrtle couldn't tell if he was being sarcastic. "Keep it under your hat, all right, Myrtle?"

"Of course," said Myrtle, offended.

"I'll be back in a bit."

The way you were dressed, Violet had noticed, tended to make you act a certain way. Violet was dressed the way she had always hated, in a fluffy white dress with a violet satin sash and trimmings of violet ribbon.

"We wanted to get some artificial violets for your hat to go with your name; wouldn't that have been darling?"

Miss Escuadrille had said. "But the shops only have yellow and red roses."

There were also itchy white stockings and some wretched little patent leather shoes called Mary Janes.

In this ridiculous getup Violet sat on one of the wire-backed chairs at a little round marble-topped table at Max Bloomstein's Pharmacy, feeling very ladylike but at the same time much younger than she was. She told Chloe everything she had overheard in the last twenty-four hours.

"If the Antis *do* think they're going to lose," Violet said, poking at the blob of vanilla ice cream in her grape ice cream soda, "they said there just won't be a quorum. What's a quorum?" She normally didn't like to ask what words meant, because it made her feel babyish, but in a costume like this, she had no choice.

"A quorum means having enough members of the legislature there to have a valid vote," said Chloe. "Sometimes dissenting state legislators will leave the state in order to prevent there being enough people to vote. It's an old trick. I'll tell Charlotte Ormond Williams we need to beef up the guard at the train station to keep them from escaping.

"At least now we know what that surprise you heard mentioned yesterday was. The publisher of the *Nashville Banner* changed sides. He used to be a Suff; now suddenly he's an Anti." Chloe shrugged. "Wonder how they got to him. Is there anything else?"

Violet thought hard. She wished she'd taken notes,

but of course that would have been too conspicuous. "I don't know. That Miss Escuadrille that I'm sharing a room with is a blithering idiot—"

"Violet," said Chloe reprovingly.

"Well, she is—she really doesn't have a clue what's going on. She just believes all the applesauce they've told her about how women are too *good* to vote or too weak or something."

"I know," said Chloe with a sigh.

"And at that meeting I went to last night, that Senator Candler, the way he was talking, I think he really *hates* females. He doesn't think we're too good to vote, he thinks we're too bad."

"I know," Chloe repeated. She was looking more tired by the minute.

"Oh, and here are these stupid pamphlets I'm supposed to be passing out at the train station this afternoon." Violet dropped the stack of leaflets on the table.

Chloe picked one up. " 'Beware! Men of the South! Heed not the song of the suffrage siren!' " She managed to get all the exclamation points in without raising her voice. Chloe had always been good at making her voice expressive. Violet thought fondly of the stories about Alaska that Chloe used to tell her.

"Read the inside," said Violet.

Chloe did and then dropped the pamphlet back on the table. "Oh, that old argument," she said. "That there are more colored women than colored men in the South, so giving women the vote will increase the colored vote.

'Save the Anglo-Saxon race!' Most of those states don't even let colored people vote anyway."

"How come there are no colored suffragists?" Violet asked.

"There are tons of colored suffragists," said Chloe. "But they've been asked to stay out of sight."

"That's not fair," said Violet. She felt she'd had a pretty thorough lifelong experience of what it was like to be seen and not heard, and being neither seen *nor* heard had to be even worse.

"Of course it isn't," said Chloe. "Drink your soda."

The bells on the door of the pharmacy jingled. A moment later Mr. Martin sat down next to them.

"Do you mind if I join you?" he said belatedly.

"Oh, hello, Theo." Chloe instantly looked less tired.

Violet studied the slowly turning wooden ceiling fans overhead while they talked. She would have liked to go somewhere else, because she was beginning to suspect that Myrtle was right and that Chloe had no intention of sending Mr. Martin to the rightabout. In fact, Chloe had probably told Mr. Martin they were going to be at the drugstore. The whole thing embarrassed Violet. She didn't understand it either, because both of the Mr. R.'s had been much better-looking and more suitable than Mr. Martin, not to mention richer. Plus they hadn't been Bolsheviks and they hadn't had Palmer agents looking for them. Violet got up and wandered over and looked at a display of boxed candies.

"What do you mean, you have to go to the movies?"

Mr. Martin was saying. "You don't even like movies! You don't like the grainy little lines running up and down the screen. They give you a headache."

"I know," said Chloe, sounding like she already had a headache. "Maybe I'll take him to the burlesque instead."

"Just who is this fella, anyway?"

"I don't know. We'll be assigned them this evening. We have to make sure the legislators have a good time so that they don't leave town over the weekend."

"Make sure they have a good time? Exactly what is that supposed to mean?"

"Theo, please. You're causing a scene."

Violet drifted farther away. She tried to interest herself in a display of Sure-Fire Liquor Cures. She was aware that everyone in the drugstore was watching Chloe and Mr. Martin quarrel, and she wished Mr. Martin would remember that there were Palmer agents looking for him.

Then she thought of something. If Mr. Martin was here, maybe Myrtle was around somewhere. Violet wanted to see her—and it would be a relief to talk to someone her own age after all the boring adult conversations she'd had to listen to lately.

Violet found Myrtle hiding in a recessed doorway beside the drugstore, under a sign advertising *Underwood Typewriters—The Machine You Will Eventually Buy.*

Myrtle was happy to see her, and they sat down on the stoop and exchanged news. Myrtle was jealous of Violet's job as a spy.

"Because it's important," Myrtle said. "I'm not doing anything important. I'm just waiting for them to vote." She nodded upward at Capitol Hill.

"You're keeping an eye on Mr. Martin," Violet pointed out. "That's important. He needs someone to keep an eye on him."

"He sure does," Myrtle agreed. "It's bad enough he has a scar on his face and three fingers missing. He doesn't need to go telling people how to change the way they do things all the time. It makes them remember him."

Violet thought Mr. Martin probably *did* need to go telling people to change the way they did things or he wouldn't be Mr. Martin. "He's in there making a scene right now," she said.

Myrtle looked apprehensive. "Maybe we should go in and stop him."

Violet shook her head. "I think that would just make it more of a scene."

Myrtle nodded, seeing the sense in this. "I don't know what's going to happen to him after this is all over. He's no good at hiding."

At the thought of "after this is all over," they both lapsed into silence. Violet was thinking about Chloe, who had yet to say that Violet could come and live with her. Violet didn't want to go home. She didn't miss it at all. All right, she missed her own room, and her bed with the green chenille spread, and her shelf full of Oz books. But she didn't miss the empty, echoing loneliness of a house with no one in it but Stephen, who wasn't really there, and Father, who never talked except to issue edicts, and Mother, who had betrayed Violet.

She supposed Myrtle was thinking about the Girls' Training Institute, and how she didn't want to go back there, and where she would go if she didn't.

"When will it all be over?" said Myrtle.

"No one knows," said Violet. "The Senate might vote on the amendment today. Or they might not, which would mean maybe they'd vote on it Monday, or maybe not. And then the House might vote on it Monday, but they have to wait for a committee to recommend it—" She broke off, noting that Myrtle was laughing at her.

"You sound like a politician or something," said Myrtle.

Violet shrugged. "'Cause I've been listening to so much political talk lately." She thought of how sick she was of political talk. "I should come visit you and Mr. Martin where you're staying, and maybe we could go—"

"No," said Myrtle.

Violet looked away, stung. A colored man in overalls was sweeping the edge of the sidewalk, his broom making gritty swishing sounds as he swept clouds of dust into the gutter.

"It's just not that interesting a place. You'd be bored," Myrtle said, sounding half apologetic.

Before Violet could reply, the door to the drugstore burst open and Mr. Martin stormed out. Violet could just imagine the eyes of everyone in the place following him and his scar and his missing fingers that the Palmer agents had such a good description of.

Myrtle jumped to her feet and waved a hasty goodbye to Violet. Violet was sorry to see her go, but Mr. Martin clearly needed supervision.

"He just refuses to understand," said Chloe when Violet sat back down at the marble-topped table. "I told him back in New York that nothing was more important than winning the vote. I don't know why he thinks I should have changed my mind now."

Violet decided this remark was not really addressed to her. "What's going to happen today?" she asked. "Are they meeting in the capitol?"

"The Senate will probably vote today," said Chloe, pulling the paper straw out of her strawberry phosphate and looking at it disconsolately. It was coming apart.

"Really? On the Susan B. Anthony Amendment?" Violet thought this was great news and couldn't understand why Chloe wasn't more excited.

"It's only the Senate," said Chloe. "That's just half of the legislature. There's still the House to worry about. And they're what we *are* worried about. We know we're going to win the Senate."

All anybody on either side ever seemed to say was that they knew they were going to win, so Violet wasn't very impressed by this. "I don't think Senator Candler is going to vote for the amendment. He despises women."

Chloe smiled and stuck her limp straw back into her drink. "No, I agree, Senator Candler will vote against it. But I still think we're going to win it. Then we'll have thirty-five and a half states, and the Antis will be more desperate than ever, and the battle will just get hotter."

Violet was relieved to see her sister smile and decided to bring up something that had been on her mind. "Chloe, when we go back to New York, can I—"

"Violet, I really can't think about that right now," said Chloe. She picked up the pamphlets. "Do you want to chuck these in the trash barrel, or shall I?"

15

The Ferocious Mrs. Catt

WITH HER WHITE DRESS AND PURPLE SATIN sash, Violet was suitably dressed to eat in the dining room at the Hermitage Hotel, and that was where she was on the evening of Saturday, August 14. The Antis must've had plenty of money, all right, because there were at least a dozen of them sitting around the dinner table. None of them seemed to make anything of the fact that Violet was there too, or to be worried about the expense.

They had had rack of lamb, tomato consommé, scalloped potatoes, creamed cauliflower, and hot slaw, and now they were waiting for dessert. The orchestra was playing, and waiters in white uniforms with white gloves were zipping to and fro carrying platters with silver covers.

Violet was being seen and not heard, just like at home, although she had long since realized that what this really meant was not being seen either. The Antis were talking about the Senate vote, which they had lost, and the House vote, which they expected to win.

"There's no way we can lose in the House," Miss Josephine Anderson Pearson said. "A week ago the Suffs had two-thirds of the House members on their side, and now, thanks to us, they haven't even got a simple majority."

"But we lost the Senate, didn't we?" said Miss Escuadrille, looking confused.

"We always expected to lose the Senate," said Miss Pearson dismissively.

"Did we expect to lose it twenty-five to four?" Miss Escuadrille asked.

"Never you mind, Annasette. Everything's under the control of wiser minds than yours," said Miss Pearson as a white-gloved waiter set a dish of caramel custard in front of her.

A week ago, Violet thought, she had telegraphed her parents from Washington. Nine days ago she had still been at home. It seemed much longer.

Mrs. James S. Pinckard looked after the waiter, who had gone to get more custard. "Nothing but white servants are visible at this hotel. They guarantee it."

"There are colored waiters downstairs in the Grill Room," said the man sitting to Violet's left, who Violet thought was named Mr. Garlick. "In fact, they're all colored."

"Oh, well, waiters." The man to Violet's right spoke, to her considerable surprise. He was dressed in a Confederate army uniform, which he had dribbled some tomato consommé down the front of. He had a bushy white mustache and long white hair combed over a bald spot on top. He had spent most of the meal staring off into space, although occasionally he stared at the other people at the table as if he was trying to figure out who they were. "People expect waiters to be colored."

Having spoken, he stared straight ahead of him again and dropped his spoon on the floor. Violet got down under the table to retrieve it for him.

"Speaking of dark colors, isn't this paneling beautiful?" said Mrs. Pinckard. "It's Circassian walnut. Made in Russia by the same factory that did the woodwork for the *Titanic.*"

"Ha, you didn't hear anything about equal rights on the *Titanic,* did you?" said Mr. Garlick. "Now what are we going to do about the Bolshevik?"

"Which Bolshevik?" said Mrs. Pinckard. "They're pretty much all Bolsheviks."

Violet had seen the spoon next to Mrs. Pinckard's high-heeled pump, but she froze and listened.

"That foreign Jew," said Mr. Garlick.

"Oh, the Jew," said Miss Pearson.

There was something about the way they both said "Jew" that made Violet's skin crawl.

"He can be made to disappear," said Mr. Garlick.

"Mr. Garlick, I really don't think we need to go as

far as *murder,*" Mrs. Pinckard whispered, and gave a nervous laugh.

Something glopped coldly down on Violet's arm. She looked. It was caramel custard. Someone must have given the Confederate veteran another spoon.

"I'm not talking about *murder,*" said Mr. Garlick, sounding both affronted and amused. "All we need is for the Jew to disappear for a week or so. That'll throw the Suffs into at least as big a tizzy as they were in when they lost Seth Walker."

"Can't they lose the Jew the same way?" said Miss Escuadrille, sounding like she was desperately trying to keep up with the conversation.

"He's not for sale," said Miss Pearson dismissively. "Do you know he actually claims to have no interest in politics? Ran for the legislature for this special session merely so he could vote for the Susan B. Anthony Amendment. No hope of making him disappear till it's over."

"Sure there is," said Mr. Garlick. "How about if he wakes up Monday morning with a big bump on his bald head, locked in the hold of a tramp steamer headed south out of New Orleans?"

Violet had heard enough. She crawled out from under the table, squeezing carefully between the Confederate veteran's gray-clad legs and Mr. Garlick's spats without touching either of them. She slid along the Circassian walnut–paneled wall and hurried through the busy lobby and out the women's entrance. She had to tell Chloe what she'd heard right away.

Chloe had been assigned to squire around a fella named Harry T. Burn, a legislator from McMinn County. He was no older than Chloe was and had had a question mark next to his name on yesterday's list. She had taken him to the burlesque and then to supper, but she must be done with him now. Violet ran down Union Street to Polk Avenue, then turned the corner and went downhill to the Tulane Hotel.

The Hope Chest was parked out front. But Chloe wasn't in her room.

"She's gone dancing with Harry T. Burn," said Miss Lewis. "They're over at the Hermitage Hotel, up on the tenth floor. I'm headed over there myself, if you'll just wait for a minute—"

"Sorry, can't," said Violet, turning and running back down the stairs again.

It was really too hot for all this running, not to mention nearly impossible in Mary Janes, which had slippery soles and narrow straps that cut into your ankle. At least the hotels were only two blocks apart. Violet walked fast, back to the ladies' entrance of the Hermitage and into the elevator, where she told the white-uniformed boy, "Top floor, please."

It took them a long time to get there, and as they rode up, Violet's panic lessened. Whoever they were talking about kidnapping—and it was clearly one of the Suff legislators—it didn't sound like a really solid plan. It was just Mr. Garlick talking, and he might be the sort of man who just liked to say things to shock people. Still, whoever they'd been talking about needed to know he might be in danger.

The elevator stopped for a long time on the eighth floor, where the Antis' hospitality suite had apparently been fully restocked. There was loud singing going on, of several anti-suffrage songs at once. None of the Antis' songs were anywhere near as stirring as the Suffs' songs, Violet thought, even when the singers weren't drunk.

The top floor of the Hermitage was a big ballroom, with a wide wooden dance floor and an orchestra. It was full of men and women—mostly women—wearing evening dress and red or yellow roses. Violet was momentarily grateful to Miss Escuadrille for dressing her in clothes that wouldn't get her thrown out of the ballroom. She looked around for her sister.

There she was—wearing a long white gown and a yellow rose and dancing with a young man with slicked-back blond hair, who was wearing a red rose.

"Miss Mayhew's certainly kept Harry T. Burn busy," said a lady standing near Violet. "If we have the woman power, we need to keep the Antis away from him. He just might be persuadable."

Persuadable or not, Mr. Burn seemed to be having a good time. Clearly Chloe was doing her work well, Violet thought. In fact, all of the men, whether they wore yellow or red roses, seemed to be enjoying the extra attention they were getting.

"I don't know, Mrs. Dudley," said another woman, whom Violet recognized as Miss Pollitzer. "He said something to me about 'my vote will never hurt you,' but he was batting his eyes when he said it. I think he's just flirting with us."

"He can flirt all he wants as long as he votes aye," said Mrs. Dudley. "Let's go get some punch."

Violet looked up to see Mr. Martin enter the ballroom. He had somehow gotten hold of a necktie and a celluloid collar, which he had buttoned over his Bolshevik soft collar, but other than that, he hadn't made any concessions to the sort of clothing you were supposed to wear in a ballroom. What was the matter with the fella, Violet thought, irritated. Why did he have to keep showing his wanted face in public?

He marched over to where Chloe was dancing with Mr. Burn. He tapped Mr. Burn on the shoulder.

"May I cut in?" Violet heard him say.

Violet knew from dancing school that there was only one way a gentleman could react to such a challenge, and that was to leave as gracefully as possible. Chloe and Mr. Martin started waltzing as Mr. Burn backed away, looking disgruntled. He headed for the sidelines, and Violet saw an Anti eyeing him eagerly. Miss Pollitzer and Mrs. Dudley were nowhere to be seen.

Violet quickly stepped into his path. "Mr. Burn,

please, may I have the honor of this dance?" She held out her hand, wondering if she should bow. The boys had been taught to do this in dancing school, but girls, of course, didn't ask people to dance. They waited to be asked. But Chloe wouldn't want Mr. Burn to fall into the hands of an Anti.

Mr. Burn looked amused. "Why not?" he said, which was not what the girls in dancing school were taught to say. He took her outstretched hand, and Violet stepped gracefully into the dance with him.

One good thing about dancing school was that even though there were about a hundred better ways to spend an afternoon, it did teach you to dance. Violet had no trouble following Mr. Burn's steps and felt only a little self-conscious waltzing across the floor among all these adults.

"I'm Violet, Miss Mayhew's sister," Violet said, introducing herself belatedly.

"And yet you seem to be on the other side," said Mr. Burn cheerfully.

"Oh, well . . . yes . . ." Violet had forgotten about the stupid red rose she was wearing.

"Your sister seems to have run into an old friend," said Mr. Burn with a sour smile.

Violet looked over at Chloe. She and Mr. Martin were standing with one arm around each other and the other hand clasped, in a waltz position, but they were no longer dancing. They were just standing there, staring at each other. No, not staring, Violet thought. Gazing. Nothing in Violet's dancing school experience had suggested that this was at all acceptable ballroom behavior. But Chloe and Mr. Martin looked as if they had forgotten that there was anyone else in the room.

"It's just someone she knew from New York," Violet said, then instantly bit her tongue. Mr. Martin was a fugitive, and giving any information about him was dangerous, even just the information that he lived in New York.

"Knew pretty well, I'd say," said Mr. Burn, and Violet was relieved that he sounded amused now instead of sour. Mr. Burn seemed like a nice man, really, Violet thought, except for being an Anti.

The waltz was coming to an end, and Violet could sense that Mr. Burn was already looking around for an older lady than Violet to dance with. And if there was one thing there was no shortage of in this ballroom, it was ladies. Violet looked around desperately. The sidelines seemed to bristle with red roses. Ah, there was a yellow rose—Miss Pollitzer! And she was nearly as pretty as Chloe, Violet thought. Behind Mr. Burn's back she gestured desperately to Miss Pollitzer, who fortunately came over to rescue Mr. Burn just as the dance ended. Miss Pollitzer was a member of the National Woman's Party, like Chloe and Alice Paul, and she knew about Violet being a spy.

"May I have the honor of this dance, Mr. Burn?" Violet heard Miss Pollitzer say.

"Delighted, I'm sure, Miss Pollitzer," said Mr. Burn, beaming. There was no question that Mr. Burn was enjoying the Susan B. Anthony Amendment very much.

Violet looked around for Chloe and Mr. Martin but couldn't see them anywhere. Well, that wouldn't do. She needed to tell Chloe about Mr. Garlick's kidnapping plan right away.

She wondered if there was anybody else she could tell. The problem was that except for Miss Pollitzer, everyone else thought she was an Anti. Mrs. Anne Dallas Dudley, the lady who'd been talking to Miss Pollitzer, was an important Nashville Suff, but if Violet spoke to her, Mrs. Dudley would assume Violet was just part of an Anti trap.

She walked over to the elevator and pushed the button. Then she lost patience and headed down the stairs.

Mr. Martin had gotten away again. He had told Myrtle to stay at home, but Myrtle, who was sick of Dead Horse Alley and of Mrs. Ready's hints that Myrtle ought to be in some sort of institute instead of traveling around with a suspicious-looking white man, followed him. They went back down Sixth Avenue toward Capitol Hill, then around the hill and along Union Street toward the Hermitage. It was Saturday night and the streets were crowded. There were white people everywhere, some with yellow or red roses and some without. Some were driving in open automobiles, stopping in the middle of the street to talk to passersby and holding up traffic. Horns honked. The music of a player piano came from an open doorway, a song that had been popular as long as Myrtle could remember:

I didn't raise my boy to be a soldier,
I brought him up to be my pride and joy.
Who dares to place a musket on his shoul-oul-der
To shoot some other mother's darling boy?

Myrtle would have liked to sing along, but she had to keep silent because she was busy turning invisible. She wove through the crowds, and no one saw her.

Then Mr. Martin went into the Hermitage. Colored people weren't allowed inside, and it was much more difficult to be invisible in places you weren't allowed to be. There was a doorman with a double row of gold buttons on his coat. Myrtle retreated. There was another entrance around the side. There was a doorman here too, but a group of suffragists with yellow ribbons on their hats went in, and Myrtle slipped silently in with them.

The desk clerk at the Hermitage was much too harassed to see Myrtle. The lobby was full of white people all talking loudly. Myrtle slid in among them, concentrating as hard as she could on being invisible. They were busy talking to each other and talking about each other. Myrtle could feel their gazes slide around her. She was doing a good job.

There was a quiet area with some potted ferns and cut-velvet sofas. It looked like a good place for Mr. Martin to be hiding. A man and a woman were sitting on one of the sofas talking, but they weren't Miss Chloe and Mr. Martin.

"I've just come from the train station, Mr. Hanover," the woman was saying. "We had to let some of the legislators leave town. After all, it's the weekend. But we're afraid that those that won't accept a bribe to change their vote might accept a bribe to just go home and stay there."

A tall, bony man with tufts of gray hair in his ears came over to them. "Joe! Evening, Miss White." He nodded vaguely at the lady. "Joe, I gotta tell you, you know that leak in my barn roof?"

Mr. Hanover looked wary and put a hand over his stomach, as though it hurt. "You have a leak in your barn roof?"

"Yeah. Well, them Antis offered me three hundred dollars to vote against ratification. You know I'm with the Suffs, Joe, I been with the Suffs since way back, but three hundred dollars . . . and with that leak in the roof . . ." He trailed off and looked at Joe hopefully.

"Three hundred dollars?" Mr. Hanover sounded outraged. "That's all they offered you? Everyone else who votes with the Antis is getting a thousand."

"A thousand?" The legislator stared. "A thousand, and they offered me a measly three hundred for my vote? Those lousy no-good Antis—what do they take me for? Forget them!"

The man stalked off, and Miss White and Mr. Hanover laughed. Myrtle would have liked to laugh too, but you couldn't do that when you were invisible. Mr. Hanover suddenly grabbed his stomach again and winced.

"Can't wait to tell Mrs. Catt about that," he said. "That was funny."

Myrtle edged carefully out into the lobby again. Mr. Martin was nowhere to be seen. He would be looking for Miss Chloe, of course. Myrtle was afraid that if she didn't manage things right, Miss Chloe was going to be Mr. Martin's downfall.

Myrtle slid along invisibly to a room that she could tell from the sounds and from the gravy smells must be the dining room. She couldn't go inside, since she didn't trust her invisibility walking right past that white-suited white headwaiter. She peered in the door as best she could. She didn't see Mr. Martin.

She slid back into the lobby. She climbed up the stone staircase to the balcony.

She had gone up there to get a better view, but the balcony was full of people wearing red roses. One woman looked directly at Myrtle. Thinking fast, Myrtle whipped out her handkerchief, dropped to her knees, and began dusting the balcony railing. At the Girls' Training Institute, they had always been sticklers for dusting railings and that sort of detail. At least that's what Myrtle remembered from the few classes she'd bothered to attend. Anyway, it worked. As soon as she started dusting, she became invisible again.

Down below, Myrtle saw Mr. Martin crossing the

lobby with Miss Chloe on his arm. They went up a little staircase to a veranda at the front of the lobby. Myrtle hurriedly pocketed her handkerchief and went back downstairs to follow them.

The veranda was made of stone, with a vaulted stone ceiling. It stretched the length of the hotel along Sixth Avenue. Down below, Myrtle could hear automobiles and a few horses passing and the voices of people in the street. There was nobody on the veranda but Mr. Martin and Miss Chloe and a very old white lady wearing an enormous hat. The old lady was approaching Miss Chloe. Myrtle moved toward them cautiously.

Just then Violet came onto the veranda and ruined everything by saying, "Hi, Myrtle!"

Everyone turned to look at Myrtle.

"Hi," said Myrtle, very annoyed.

"What is this?" the old lady demanded.

"Mrs. Catt, this is my friend Theo Martin," said Miss Chloe, looking tired. "And my sister, Violet, and her little friend Myrtle."

"Your sister seems to be an Anti," said Mrs. Catt.

"I'm not an Anti, Mrs. Catt," said Violet, covering her red rose with her hand. "I'm just wearing this. In fact, I wanted to tell Chloe—"

"Preposterous!" said Mrs. Catt. "*Just* wearing the anti-suffrage rose? Do you have any idea how many women have lived their whole lives—yes, and died too!—for your right to vote? And you're *just* wearing an anti-suffrage rose?"

Mr. Martin looked at the old lady with interest. "You

must be Carrie Chapman Catt. I would be honored to shake your hand."

He grabbed her hand and shook it, which Myrtle thought was brave of him, considering the way Mrs. Catt was glaring at him.

"You're a Bolshevik, aren't you?" said Mrs. Catt. She turned to Miss Chloe. "We do not need this, Miss Mayhew!" Mrs. Catt said. "We do not need anarchists and—and Negroes!"

"I'm not an anarchist," said Mr. Martin. "I'm a socialist."

"I don't know about you, Mrs. Catt," said Miss Chloe coldly. "But I'm fighting for the right to vote for Negroes too."

Myrtle felt a sudden rush of affection for Miss Chloe.

"Fine," Mrs. Catt said. "But that doesn't mean you have to parade your little colored friend around now and scare these old Confederates in the legislature out of voting for suffrage. Do you know what a legislator from Mississippi told me?"

There was silence.

"He told me," Mrs. Catt went on, "that the reason he was opposed to woman suffrage was that the white men in Mississippi beat up any Negro man who tries to vote and that he didn't really like the idea of having to beat up a woman. 'Not even a black one,' he said."

Myrtle stared at Mrs. Catt. She couldn't tell if Mrs. Catt thought this was a bad thing, or a good thing, or just a thing that was.

"So keep your little colored friends and Bolsheviks hidden, please, until after the vote. Do you know how long we've fought to reach this moment? Seventy-two years!" Mrs. Catt said. "Seventy-two years, do you hear me? And now, at the scene of the final battle, you play games, you wear the enemy's colors, you treat the culmination of our years of sacrifice as if it were nothing more than a game of, a game of . . ."

She seemed at a loss to say what kind of game it was, and Myrtle wasn't about to suggest one. Mrs. Catt was a frightening old lady.

"Chloe, I really need to tell you something," said Violet. "I beg your pardon," she added as an afterthought. Myrtle had noticed that Violet's well-bred manners had been steadily deteriorating ever since they'd met. Personally, Myrtle thought this was a great improvement in Violet. What Myrtle knew about white people with well-bred manners was that they required servants to wait on them, and Myrtle was against that.

Violet looked at Mrs. Catt as if trying to decide whether she could be trusted and then apparently decided she could, on what grounds Myrtle couldn't imagine. Violet hurriedly gabbled out something about a plot to kidnap one of the Suff legislators, although she wasn't sure which one.

"Mr. Hanover," said Mrs. Catt promptly. "Our floor leader in the House. He needs a bodyguard. I've been saying that all along. I'll have Mrs. Dudley talk to Governor Roberts about it immediately."

"Is he really a foreign Bolshevik?" said Violet, interested.

"No, he's a lawyer from Memphis," said Mrs. Catt. "But I believe he came from Poland as a child."

"Who was this fella you said you heard talking about it?" said Miss Chloe.

"Someone named Mr. Garlick," said Violet. "I hadn't seen him before tonight."

"A mystery man," said Mrs. Catt grimly. "We've run into the mystery men in every single state. They always show up when the legislature is debating the Susan B. Anthony Amendment. Nobody ever knows where they come from."

A hotel bellhop came out on the veranda. "Excuse me, ladies," he said, then his eyes rested on Myrtle. "I beg your pardon, but we don't allow colored people in the hotel."

"Come along, Myrtle," said Mr. Martin. "Excuse us, ladies."

"I'll go talk to Mrs. Dudley now about that bodyguard," said Chloe.

"After you do that, let's all go out for ice cream," Mr. Martin suggested.

"In the alley," Myrtle muttered as she followed Violet and him off the veranda.

16

Politics and Gunplay

IN VIOLET'S OPINION, SUNDAY WAS AN ALMOST normal day. They packed a picnic lunch of sliced chicken sandwiches, pickles, and Chero-Cola and rode in the Hope Chest out to a quiet field beside a river where there was nobody around to worry about what any of them looked like. They didn't wear any roses either. Violet and Myrtle rode in the wooden truck bed on the back of the Hope Chest. It was a bumpy, dusty ride, but Violet didn't care because she was wearing her horrible plaid dress and she was hoping to ruin it.

She did, too. Chloe insisted that the first thing you had to learn about cars was how to take care of them, so she brought out a grease gun and an oilcan and showed Myrtle and Violet how to lubricate the spindle bolt and the steering ball socket and the universal joint and about a hundred other things Violet couldn't remember the names of. While the three of them climbed over and under the Hope Chest, getting gloriously dirty, Mr. Martin sat under a tree and read the Sunday paper.

Then Chloe showed them how to start the thing. Violet doubted she'd ever be able to start a car by herself. It seemed to require two people: one to turn the crank at the front (which was tricky, because if the car backfired, the crank could break your arm, said Chloe) and one to work the throttle and the spark, two levers on the steering wheel. And you had to really listen, said Chloe. Violet didn't know what Chloe was really listening for, because when the thing started, it sounded like a barrel of tin cans being eaten by a steam engine.

To drive the car, you had to use your feet to work the reverse pedal and the high- and low-speed clutch and your hand to work the throttle. It was too much to think of all at once, and Violet was glad that they had this whole big open field so that she didn't have to worry too much about steering. Instead, she concentrated on using the foot pedals and hand levers to keep the car running as it jolted and jumped over the hummocky field.

When it was Myrtle's turn to drive, Violet went to sit with Mr. Martin and look at the newspaper. Mr. Martin had prudently moved a little farther into the trees, out of the way of the Hope Chest.

"Is the whole Sunday paper about nothing but baseball?" Violet asked, flipping through the pages.

"Pretty much. Isn't it grand?"

"Why is there nothing in here about what's going on with the amendment?" Violet asked.

"They're probably trying to pretend it isn't happening," said Mr. Martin. "Good heavens, I can't believe the Yankees lost to the Tigers. They should never have taken on Babe Ruth."

Violet noticed a story at the top of the page. "They caught him!"

Mr. Martin started. "Caught who?" he said warily.

"'Veteran hobo at twelve is in hands of police,'" Violet read aloud. "Hobie. The fella who helped us get to Washington."

"Poor lad," said Mr. Martin. "But he'll be off on his travels again soon, I'm sure."

Violet read the article. The reporter seemed very amused by the whole story and recounted that Hobie claimed he'd be off again in no time.

"Looks like the White Sox are getting stomped," Mr. Martin observed. "They deserve it after last year."

Violet looked up at Myrtle and Chloe bumping over the field in the Hope Chest (Myrtle, who was shorter than Violet, seemed to be having considerable difficulty seeing over the hood while working both the hand and foot controls) and then at Mr. Martin reading baseball scores. They all had something hanging over them, Violet thought. Myrtle had nowhere to go except back to the Girls' Training Institute. Poor Mr. Martin seemed to have nowhere to go but jail. And what about Chloe?

Violet wasn't sure if Chloe saw anything after the Tennessee vote at all.

Later she and Myrtle took off their shoes and stockings and waded in a creek at the bottom of the field. The water was pleasantly cool on their feet, and little minnows came up and nibbled on their legs as they stood in the current. Violet told Myrtle about Hobie being caught and sent home to his stepmother.

"He'll take off again," said Myrtle. "Probably already has."

"Do you ever think about what you're going to do with the rest of your life, Myrtle?" said Violet.

"Yes," said Myrtle.

"Well, what?" said Violet.

"I don't know. But it's going to be important," said Myrtle.

They walked farther downstream and tried to catch some frogs. When Violet finally did catch one, she held it for a moment, enjoying the cool feel of its soft clammy skin in her hands, and then it pushed off with its mighty hind legs and plopped into the water. Violet asked Myrtle if it wasn't time they headed back, and Myrtle said it wasn't, so they walked even farther downstream and talked about the things they'd seen and done and heard in Nashville.

Violet wanted to know more about where Myrtle and Mr. Martin were staying, but Myrtle was curiously reluctant to talk about it.

"It's called Dead Horse Alley," said Myrtle. "We're staying with a lady in her house."

"Is it like the alleys in Washington?" said Violet, remembering the tumbledown shacks and heaps of trash and rats.

"Sort of different," said Myrtle with a shrug. "Look, there's some kind of animal hole over here."

So they went over to the bank and looked at a burrow under the roots of a willow tree and tried to decide what might live there. Myrtle was fun to explore with, Violet thought, a lot more fun than the Antis. But the world seemed to have been set up so that Myrtle and Violet would always be on different sides of an invisible line.

By Monday, August 16, nobody could tell which side anybody was on anymore. Nobody knew when the House was going to vote. The Antis and the Suffs were both polling the legislators every few hours, and it seemed like every few hours the list of who was an Anti and who was a Suff had changed. Chloe told Violet at their noon meeting that she didn't think the polls were good at all anymore.

They had met at the lunchroom in Union Station because Violet was supposed to have been spending the morning watching the train station telegraph offices for the Antis. She hadn't really been doing this, of course, but she had gone down to the train station for verisimilitude.

Chloe had been assigned to spend some more time with Harry T. Burn, but he had gone up to the capitol. The Suffs' strategy required that only Tennessee women lobby legislators at the capitol. Northerners were known to irritate Southerners, and the Suffs didn't want the Tennessee legislators to be irritated.

"I don't think we have a chance with Burn anyway," said Chloe. "He's just enjoying the attention. He's so young." Violet had heard that Burn was twenty-four, which was a year older than Chloe. "He's still wearing a red rose."

"Let's go up to the capitol," said Chloe when they finished their chicken salad sandwiches.

"But we're not supposed to," said Violet.

"Oh, we won't lobby anybody," said Chloe. "I just want to see what's going on. Besides, you've never seen inside it, have you? It's nice."

Chloe drove the Hope Chest carefully along Broadway and then up Sixth Avenue, braking to let people pass. The city seemed to be getting more crowded every minute. Not everyone had yellow or red symbols to show that they were Suffs or Antis—there were a lot of tourists who had just come to watch the battle. Chloe stopped to let a woman pushing a high-backed wicker wheelchair cross the street. In the wheelchair was a young man whose legs ended at the knee, who Violet guessed from his age might've been a soldier. The woman looked like she might be his mother.

"I wish you hadn't left Stephen alone like that," Chloe said.

"You wish *I* hadn't!" Violet was stung by the unfairness

of this. "I didn't leave him alone; I left him with Mother and Father."

"Yes, but being with Mother and Father can be a bit like being alone, you know."

"Yes, I do know, as a matter of fact," Violet said, folding her arms.

"Violet, you don't think I abandoned you, do you? Father threw me out."

"No, he didn't," Violet argued. "He told you never to darken his door again when you bought the Hope Chest, but you'd already moved out by then."

"Yes." Chloe stopped again; a yellow dog was wandering across the road ahead of them. "I had to leave, Violet."

"So did I," said Violet. "Anyway, it's not like Stephen really notices who's around him."

"I think he does," said Chloe.

Then Violet remembered that Chloe had studied to be a nurse since leaving home. "Do people with shell shock ever get better?"

"Some do," said Chloe. "It takes time. And it may be that they all do—it's a fairly new disease; we don't know much about it. Damn!" The engine gave a loud *pow* and stopped running. "Now we're stalled. Violet, could you crank?"

Violet got out, went to the front of the car, and inserted the metal crank that turned the starter. She cranked until the car coughed, spat smoke, and started.

Then she got back in the passenger seat next to Chloe. They chugged on.

"So what causes it, then?" Violet said.

"Well, some doctors believe it's caused by low air pressure in areas where a lot of shells have been fired."

"Not by . . ." Violet searched for a word.

"Cowardice?" said Chloe bluntly. "No, why should it be? After all, shell shock is a new disease, and cowardice is as old as humanity."

Violet thought about this. It made sense. That was one of the nice things about Chloe: she was always so sensible.

Then Chloe ruined it by saying, "Violet, even if Stephen *was* frightened, why shouldn't he be? Surrounded by bombs and bullets and enemy soldiers?"

Violet made no reply. She liked the low-air-pressure explanation better.

The street in front of the capitol was full of Model Ts, parked diagonally on both sides. Chloe slid the Hope Chest into an empty space and they got out.

Violet remembered her red rose and pulled it off, sticking it inside her hat in case she needed it later. "Doesn't it matter, us going into the capitol together when I'm pretending to be an Anti?" she asked.

"I don't think anyone's paying any attention at this point," said Chloe with a tired smile. "Both sides are panicking, just trying to figure out which side the legislators are on and when the vote is going to happen.

"There are some Tennessee Suffs up here guarding the special House committee that's supposed to meet on the amendment tonight." Chloe nodded up at the capitol.

"What's the committee meeting supposed to do?" Violet asked as they climbed up the seventy-two stone steps toward the capitol. Violet had heard that a Model T Ford had climbed these steps a few years ago to prove the superiority of automobiles to horse-drawn carriages. Violet wondered if Chloe would be willing to try driving the Hope Chest up these steps. She looked at Chloe's exhausted face and decided now was not the time to suggest it.

"A committee's job is to look at a bill and decide whether or not to send it to the floor to be voted on by the legislature," Chloe said, sounding weary. "In this case, it's a bill saying that Tennessee ratifies the Susan B. Anthony Amendment." She stopped to rest, leaning against the pedestal of a statue. "A week ago we had a clear majority; nearly two-thirds of the House members said they favored the bill. But thanks to the Antis and their businessmen and mystery men, it now looks like the committee might not even vote to send the bill to the floor."

"And if it does get sent to the floor," said Violet, moving around to see if there was any shade anywhere, "then it needs a three-fourths vote to pass?"

"Three-fourths? No, no. Only a majority. More than half of the House, that's all it needs."

"In school we learned . . ." Violet frowned, trying to remember. It hadn't seemed nearly as important when they'd learned it in school as it did now. "A constitutional amendment requires a two-thirds vote of Congress and three-fourths of the state legislatures."

"That means the legislatures of three-fourths of the states," said Chloe. "In other words, thirty-six of the forty-eight states. And we've got thirty-five and a half now. But we don't need the Tennessee House itself to vote three-fourths in favor. All we need is a simple majority. And we're so close." She looked up at the old cannons that surrounded the capitol, left over from the Civil War.

"Capitols are built on hills so they can be protected if the people revolt," said Chloe, looking up at the cannons and smiling.

Violet guessed from the smile that Chloe had probably heard this from Mr. Martin.

"Why are the women Antis even bothering?" Violet asked. This had been on her mind for the last several days. "If they're that much against voting, why don't they just not vote when they get the right?"

"Some people are never satisfied unless they're making choices for other people," said Chloe. "And of course a lot of the Antis are funded by big business and by the political machines. Politics in this country is very corrupt, you know, Violet. Most elections are bought and sold. People sell their votes, and political machines in each city and state organize the purchase of votes."

Violet nodded, too out of breath from the heat and the climbing to bother replying.

"The corrupt bosses don't want women to mess things up," Chloe went on. "They've spent over a century building up the vote-buying system they've got now, and everything is so fine-tuned. If twenty-seven million voters are suddenly added to the rolls for the November election, it will destroy all their calculations."

Violet moved around the statue again, still trying to find a spot of shade. "Who was this fella?"

Chloe squinted up at the statue. "Edward Ward Carmack. He was a newspaper editor who was gunned down in the streets of Nashville a few years ago. His murderers were pardoned by the governor—not the governor they have now."

"Pardoned by the governor?" Violet tried to look up at the statue silhouetted against the blazing white sun but couldn't. "They shot him down in the street in cold blood and they were *pardoned by the governor*?"

"Well, I don't know if it was cold blood," said Chloe, patting the pedestal. "Mr. Carmack might have drawn first. But in his newspaper he'd criticized the men who shot him, and he'd also criticized Governor Patterson. He was against the liquor interests, Mr. Carmack was, and Patterson was for them. Governor Patterson pardoned the killers before they'd spent a day in jail."

"So the governor of a state can just have people he doesn't like killed?" Violet said. Nothing she had learned about government in school had suggested this.

"Oh, I doubt it was quite like that," Chloe said. "Come on."

As they climbed on, Violet looked back at the statue, suddenly struck with the idea that messing around in politics could be a deadly business. The liquor interests hadn't liked Mr. Carmack, and they didn't like suffragists either. In spite of the midday heat, Violet shivered.

Inside the capitol the low, vaulted stone ceilings gave you the feeling you were underground. It was dark and felt cooler than outside. They climbed a wide stone staircase. Violet ran her hand over the cool stone handrail. There was a huge, jagged-looking gouge out of it. But when Violet touched it, she found that it too was smooth, as if hands had worn it down for many years.

Chloe noticed Violet looking at it. "That's from a bullet," she said. "When the Tennessee legislature met after the Civil War, some of the legislators tried to escape because they didn't want to vote for Tennessee to rejoin the Union. But there were soldiers guarding them, and they opened fire."

Violet stared at the gouge in the stair rail. "No wonder Father thinks politics isn't safe for women!"

Chloe laughed. "Well, I like to think once we're in, there'll be a little less gunplay involved. Anyway, you can see why the Tennessee legislators might still be a little persnickety about having Yankees in here telling them what to do."

"Yes," said Violet. She followed Chloe up the stairs.

The second story was lighter, with a high stone

ceiling. The hallway was shaped like a cross. At one end was the House of Representatives, and at the other were the Senate and the library.

It all seemed oddly quiet after all the fuss and noise in the Hermitage and in the streets and in the train station during the last week.

"Thank goodness you're here, Miss Mayhew!" Miss Pollitzer burst through a doorway. "We need to work on two of the Suff committee members, quick. We've lost them."

"I thought only Southern women were allowed to lobby with legislators here in the capitol," Chloe said.

"They're not in the capitol. I mean we've *lost* them," said Miss Pollitzer. "Blotz and Credwell. They've flown the coop. Do you know what they look like?"

"I think so," said Chloe.

"Then go, please. Look for them. We've got search parties out. Mrs. Anne Dallas Dudley has gone to the Hermitage and Miss Sue Shelton White is searching the moving picture shows and Skalowski's Ice Cream Parlor. We have guards covering the train station, and I'm going down to check the Interurban station on Broadway, but Credwell might have an automobile. We need someone to drive out the highway looking for them. Is the Hope Chest nearby?"

Myrtle and Mr. Martin were trying a variation on their diet of sardines, Uneeda biscuits, and peaches. Myrtle had gotten a can of tuna fish instead. Myrtle was setting the Uneeda biscuits neatly out on a napkin on Mrs. Ready's oilcloth tabletop and Mr. Martin was just slicing through the lid of the tuna fish can with his pocketknife when the door burst open. It hit the wall with a loud crack, and a board fell off it and clattered to the floor.

Two men pounced into the room. They both had guns out, pointed at Mr. Martin. Myrtle dove into a corner.

"Don't move, Arpadfi," one of the men barked.

Mr. Martin raised his hands over his head. "I'm not Arpadfi."

"Of course you are. Who else would be able to pronounce it? Drop the knife. And that device you're holding in your game hand."

Mr. Martin dropped the knife and the tuna fish on the floor. The knife stuck in the wooden floor. The can rolled lopsidedly, a smell of tuna fish rising from the oil dribbling out.

The men peered at the can intently. "Not a bomb. Just a can of tuna fish," one of them announced. "Cover him, Hank. I'm gonna put the cuffs on him."

The man who had spoken moved over behind Mr. Martin, grabbed his hands, and jerked them down behind Mr. Martin's back. Myrtle winced in sympathy. It was what that evil brakeman had done to her on the freight train.

"Don't try nothing funny," said Hank. "Nobody cares if we shoot dangerous alien radicals."

"I'm not an alien," said Mr. Martin. "I'm a U.S. citizen."

"Uh-huh. And just when did you become a U.S. citizen, Arpadfi?"

"My name is Theodore Martin, and I was born in the United States."

"Let's drop the Martin bushwa, okay? You're Sandor Arpadfi, you were born in some European hellhole or other—"

"Hungary," the other agent put in.

"Hungary, then, around 1892, and you came to the United States in 1897. You lost three fingers in an industrial accident in 1898 and your left eye in a knife fight in 1916." The man who was holding Mr. Martin's arms—he had handcuffs hanging at his belt, Myrtle noticed, but he made no move to get them—traced the scar from Mr. Martin's eye downward with his finger. It must be a glass eye, Myrtle realized. Mr. Martin jerked his head away.

"Resisting arrest," the agent commented, twisting Mr. Martin's arms more tightly behind his back.

"It wasn't a 'knife fight,'" said Mr. Martin through clenched teeth. "The other man had a knife. I did not. And I am a U.S. citizen."

"Right, you became a citizen in 1913," said the agent. "In other words, after you'd already become a radical. A radical can't become a U.S. citizen. I think the courts will find that your citizenship oath is null and void."

"That's insane!" Mr. Martin protested. Drops of sweat stood out on his forehead. Having his arms twisted must have hurt a lot, but he was trying not to show it. That was being brave, Myrtle supposed, but she wished he would cry out in pain so that his captors would be satisfied and stop hurting him.

"In your position, I wouldn't go calling the laws of the United States of America insane," the agent suggested.

"I don't believe that is the law," Mr. Martin panted. "And if it is the law, then it is insane."

"Did you hear that, Hank?" the agent asked.

"Sure did, Christopher," said Hank. "Anything else you want to tell us about the laws of the United States, Arpadfi?"

Mr. Martin glared at both of them and would have liked to say a lot of things, Myrtle could tell. "Only that I'm as much a citizen of the USA as you are, and I know my rights."

"You're a member of a radical organization and you don't have no rights," said Hank smugly.

"I'm a member of a labor union," said Mr. Martin. "It's my"—he gasped in pain and Myrtle winced again—"First Amendment right."

"The International Workers of the World is a labor union the way the Boston Tea Party was a tea party," Christopher said. "Quit arguing with us or we might notice you pulled a knife on us. You see how he had that knife out when we came in, Hank?"

He kicked at the open pocketknife where it had fallen on the floor. Myrtle would have liked to grab it and put it away, but then they'd probably say she'd pulled it on them.

"Sure did," said Hank. "You gonna come along quietly, Arpadfi, or should we report you pulled a knife on us?"

Mr. Martin looked deflated, the same way he had on the train when he'd argued with the conductor, Myrtle thought. "What choice do I have? I am coming along quietly."

He looked at Myrtle as if he was about to say something. Myrtle shook her head and put a finger to her lips to silence him. It was better for both of them if Myrtle remained invisible.

In spite of the fact that Mr. Martin was coming along quietly, the agents seemed to find it necessary to do quite a bit of kicking and shoving to get him out the door. Myrtle turned away. She picked up the knife Mr. Martin or Arpadfi or whatever his name was had dropped, folded it, and stuck it in the pocket of her blue dress next to her picture of Mama and Daddy. She went to the cot where she slept and grabbed her toothbrush. She was just heading out the door when she bumped into Mrs. Ready coming in.

"Got him, did they?" said Mrs. Ready. "Thank the good Lord. Child, now that you're free of that horrible man, I'm taking you to Mrs. Frankie Pierce. She's a colored suffragist leader who's done wonders in finding institutions that will take in wayward colored girls, and I'm sure she'll find—"

Mrs. Ready was packing up Myrtle's bundle as she said all this, and Myrtle didn't wait around to hear the rest of it. She didn't know if Mrs. Ready had turned in Mr. Martin—lots of people could have done it, he'd been so careless about staying hidden—and she wasn't about to ask her. If Mrs. Ready had done it, then she'd have to hate Mrs. Ready, and she really didn't have time for that. She ran out the door.

17

The Hope Chest

"WHY WOULD THEY RUN AWAY?" VIOLET asked as she and Chloe dashed back down the stone steps of Capitol Hill. "If they're against the amendment, why not just vote 'no'?"

"Because they promised us their votes," Chloe explained breathlessly. It was much too hot for all this running. "And it's easier to run away than to go back on a promise."

Fortunately, the Hope Chest started after a few turns of its crank. Violet was just climbing into the passenger seat when Myrtle came running up, out of breath and holding a toothbrush in her hand.

"Violet! Miss Chloe! Mr. Martin!"

"Calm down, dear," Chloe suggested.

Myrtle shook her head. "They've arrested Mr. Martin!"

Chloe went pale. "Who?"

"Agents," said Myrtle. "They hit him and told him he wasn't an American."

"Violet, turn the car off and wait here," Chloe said. She followed Myrtle, and both of them went charging off down Union Street.

Violet watched them go. Should she follow them? No. She was worried about Mr. Martin, but whatever there was to be done for him, Chloe and Myrtle were going to do. Chloe had told Violet to wait here. But someone had to search the highway for Blotz and Credwell. The Suffs were counting on Chloe and Violet to do it.

Could she do it? She'd only driven the Hope Chest once before, with Chloe sitting next to her to tell her what to do. Well, never mind—she could do it. She had to.

It was a good thing the Hope Chest was still running, because Violet doubted she could have started the thing by herself. She moved over into the driver's seat. She sat as tall as she could so that she could see over the hood, and she stretched her legs to reach the pedals. She breathed in the smell of burning gasoline. She looked down at the pedals on the floor. *R* for reverse. She kicked the pedal. The Hope Chest gave an anguished cough, as though it was about to stall, and Violet grabbed the throttle and gave it some gas. The car shot backward. A horse whinnied in fear. Violet stamped on the pedal marked *B* for brake and grabbed at the steering wheel. Terrified, she turned and looked behind her. The horse was making good its escape, its rider clinging to its back, but she'd come within an inch of hitting a parked Hupmobile.

Violet gripped the steering wheel so hard that if it had been alive, it would have screamed. Resolutely she stamped on the clutch to move the car forward and then, carefully, touched the throttle and gave it some gas. The Hope Chest lunged like a racehorse breaking from a starting gate. Several pedestrians scattered out of Violet's way.

She didn't remember the car going this fast when she drove it with Chloe. But the paved street offered less resistance than the grassy field. The car surged down the street. Violet clasped the steering wheel tightly and concentrated on staying in the exact middle of the street. She knew you were supposed to drive on the right, but that looked too difficult. There were so many things a person could hit on the side of the road, cars and lampposts and people. She thudded over the trolley tracks. The thing was going much too fast, and she wasn't even touching the throttle. She half stood, trying to see the road better. She seemed to be hurtling at things and people on both sides, and each time she cranked the steering wheel to avoid something, something else sprang up in her path. She couldn't imagine why anyone would want to drive a car—this was horrible, like a nightmare.

She was supposed to turn left up here, she knew, to get to the highway. But how did you slow down to turn? She cranked the steering wheel to the left and the Hope Chest veered wildly, rocking onto two wheels and then hitting the pavement again hard.

"Reduce the spark!" a woman screamed at her from the sidewalk. Out of the corner of her eye, Violet noticed that a lot of people were staring at her.

Violet looked down to find the lever on the steering wheel that controlled the spark, and the Hope Chest climbed up onto the sidewalk. People fled, screaming.

"I'm sorry!" Violet yelled as she got the car back onto the road and got the spark down. Now the Hope Chest was much quieter and didn't seem to want to go as fast. It coasted slowly to a stop, coughed, belched out a cloud of burned-smelling black smoke, and almost stalled before Violet grabbed the throttle lever and it jumped forward again. This time she kept her eyes on the road and kept driving right down the middle.

"I don't care what anyone says," she heard a woman on the sidewalk say. "There ought to be a law against children driving those things."

She had the hang of it now. The important thing was to keep moving, because otherwise the Hope Chest might stall and she knew she couldn't start it again. And that none of the agitated crowd on the sidewalk would help her.

"Which way to the highway?" she called.

Several people pointed, and someone called, "Left at the corner and take your second right!"

Behind her, Violet heard a bell clanging angrily. It was

a trolley car. Violet was driving right down the trolley track in the middle of the street. She looked over to the side, where she was supposed to drive, but the space looked too dangerously narrow. Well, the trolley would just have to follow her.

Soon Violet had left the trolley track and the city behind, and the Hope Chest was bouncing merrily along a rutted dirt road into the country. Violet could see why Chloe liked the Hope Chest so much. This was glorious. It made you feel free. As if you had no bonds at all. Nothing to hold you back from going wherever you wanted and doing whatever you felt needed to be done.

She saw a car up ahead on the edge of the dusty highway. She took her hand off the throttle and slowed down.

A cream-colored Oakland Sensible Six was stopped beside the road, and a man was kneeling in the dust beside it, staring at a rear wheel. Violet pulled up beside the Oakland and stopped the Hope Chest carefully, not letting it stall.

The man looked up. He was in his forties and had rather the seedy look of a drummer, perhaps because he'd left his hat on although he'd taken off his jacket and pulled his sleeves up under his sleeve garters.

"Are you Mr. Credwell or Mr. Blotz?" Violet called to him.

"Beg pardon?" said the man, standing up and brushing dust off his knees. "You'll have to turn that thing off. I can't hear you."

With a sigh of regret, Violet let the Hope Chest stall. "Are you Mr. Credwell or Mr. Blotz?"

The man tipped his hat politely. "Credwell. Got a flat. And me without a spare."

Well, that was one of the runaway legislators found, anyway. "Where's Blotz?" she said.

"I don't know," said Mr. Credwell, shrugging.

"The committee's about to meet to vote on whether to send the ratification bill to the floor," Violet said. "You're supposed to be there to vote!"

"Oh, is it?" Mr. Credwell looked off into the middle distance. "I guess it was in my memorandum book, but I must've forgotten to look at it."

Violet almost pounded the steering wheel in frustration. Did this man have no idea how much his vote mattered to Chloe? And to women who had to wait in train stations for their son's coffins to come home from France and to a few million other people, including, now that Violet thought about it, herself? "Mr. Credwell, please come back to town at once."

Mr. Credwell shuffled his feet in the dust with the guilty look of a boy caught skipping school. "Sure. I was just headed back." His car was pointed the other way.

Mr. Credwell chivalrously offered to turn the crank to start the Hope Chest. Violet worked the levers. It took them quite a while to get the thing started, because she didn't have a good ear for it yet.

"You know why they call it a runabout, don't you?" said Mr. Credwell.

Violet had heard this one before, but they were all supposed to do their best to keep the legislators in a good mood, so she said, "Why?"

"Because it'll run about a mile before it breaks down, ha ha!" said Mr. Credwell.

Violet smiled politely. "Ha ha. Please get in, Mr. Credwell."

"Do you, er, mind if I drive, Miss, er . . ."

"Miss Mayhew," said Violet. "And yes, I do."

Mr. Credwell humbly climbed into the Hope Chest and permitted himself to be driven back into town. He asked Violet to stop at a garage so he could get a spare, so Violet did. But once he'd got it, she went right on driving back to the capitol.

Miss Pollitzer had caught the other legislator, Blotz, trying to escape on the Interurban, the electric train system that connected cities from the East Coast to the Mississippi.

That night the committee voted 10–8 to send the Susan B. Anthony Amendment to the floor. Without Mr. Blotz and Mr. Credwell, Violet realized, the vote would have been tied.

The next day, Tuesday, August 17, Violet did not see Chloe or Myrtle at all. Everyone thought the amendment would be voted on that day. Violet went to their usual noon meeting place at Max Bloomstein's Pharmacy, but Chloe did not show up. Violet slowly sipped a chocolate phosphate through a paper straw and worried. What if they had arrested Chloe too? Why would they, though? Chloe hadn't done anything. But then, according to Chloe, all Mr. Martin had done was speak out against the War, so who knew what people could get arrested for? And anyway, Chloe had been in jail before.

The door jangled seventeen times before the last of the phosphate gurgled in the bottom of Violet's glass, but it was never Chloe. With a sigh, Violet got up and left. On the way back to the Hermitage, Violet heard a newsboy hollering that some baseball player had been hit by a fast pitch and killed. That would upset Mr. Martin, Violet thought. If he ever even heard about it, that is. Who knew where he was being kept or what was being done to him or to Chloe or to Myrtle?

Turning these worries over in her head, Violet walked across the sweltering lobby of the Hermitage and heard someone calling her name.

She was surprised to see it was Mr. Hanover, the non-Bolshevik Jewish lawyer from Memphis who was leading the House fight. Imagine him remembering her name. She was glad (and slightly proud of herself) to see that Mr. Hanover had no bump on his head and had not been locked in the hold of a slow freighter heading south out of New Orleans.

"How do you do, Mr. Hanover?" she said politely. She looked curiously at the enormous blond man standing just behind Mr. Hanover's shoulder. Governor Roberts had indeed gotten Mr. Hanover a bodyguard—a huge one.

"Fine, fine," said Mr. Hanover. "Actually, I think I'm

getting an ulcer, but that's neither here nor there. Listen, could you tell your sister that she doesn't need to bother with Mr. Ezekiel? I heard she was looking for him, but Mr. Ezekiel's ours. In fact, I'll tell you a funny story—"

Violet had already heard from Myrtle the story of how Mr. Ezekiel had told Mr. Hanover the Antis had offered him $300 for his vote and had tried to get Mr. Hanover to offer him more. But she hadn't heard it from Mr. Hanover, so she laughed politely. Mr. Hanover was a nice fella. In spite of his baldness, he really wasn't much older than Chloe. About Mr. Martin's age, maybe. Violet suddenly felt that there was something really good about people who fought for the rights of other people, and she wished there was some way she could tell Mr. Hanover that.

"Mr. Hanover, I'm not really an Anti. And thank you." She unpinned the red rose from her dress and handed it to Mr. Hanover (keeping the pin because it would ruin the gesture if she stabbed him in the hand).

She supposed Mr. Hanover must've known she wasn't an Anti or he wouldn't have told her the story. But she felt better for saying it anyway. She wondered why Mr. Hanover thought Chloe had been looking for Mr. Ezekiel . . . she couldn't remember ever seeing a question mark next to Mr. Ezekiel's name.

She went back up to her room. It was sweltering hot. Miss Escuadrille was laundering her bloomers in the washbasin. Violet turned on the fan—she didn't care whether Miss Escuadrille minded or not—and flopped down on the bed.

"There you are." Miss Escuadrille came out of the bathroom and hung a pair of black bloomers on the line she'd strung. "You know the House might vote today? We're all supposed to go up there and show the colors. Where's your rose?"

"I'm not wearing it anymore," said Violet. "I'm for woman suffrage, Miss Escuadrille."

Surprisingly, Miss Escuadrille took this in stride. "You know, I'm beginning to wonder if I might be too. I was saying to myself, you know, Annasette, you're not even married, so all this queen of the household applesauce doesn't really apply to you anyway—"

"You didn't say that to yourself, I said it to you," said Violet irritably.

"It's not only that, you know," Miss Escuadrille went on as if Violet had not spoken. "There are probably lots of women who are married and they're still not queens of the household, or maybe the household they're the queen of is some one-room shack with no floor beside the railroad track, and maybe it's really not my business to decide whether they should vote or not. And anyway, who's to say I wouldn't do a good job of voting once I set my mind to it?"

Violet stared at Miss Escuadrille as if she had sprouted horns.

"Did you just change sides?" she asked Miss Escuadrille.

Miss Escuadrille gave her a bewildered look. "You know, I think I did."

She shook out another pair of bloomers and hung them up.

In the evening there was an Anti party on the mezzanine. The Antis were celebrating because the North Carolina legislature had rejected the Susan B. Anthony Amendment. Violet went for the refreshments. But she didn't wear a red rose, and she didn't bother to pretend she was an Anti anymore. She went as herself.

"Here's to North Carolina!" Miss Josephine Anderson Pearson cried, lifting a glass of grape lemonade high beside the Confederate flag on the wall.

"Hear, hear!"

"May Tennessee follow in her footsteps!" said Mrs. Pinckard.

"They didn't actually vote it down," a woman near Violet said conversationally. "They voted to table it till next year."

"Oh, really?" said Violet politely, eating her pineapple ice.

"We might do the same," said the woman. "If it looks like we're going to lose, which just between you and me and the barn gate . . ."

"I want the Susan B. Anthony Amendment to pass," Violet said.

The woman looked at her in surprise. "Young lady!

That would be the worst thing that could happen to American womanhood."

"Why?" said Violet. "I can think of lots worse things that can happen to American womanhood. Like right now, when we're taxed but not represented, and we can go to jail for breaking laws we didn't pass." She thought of Chloe, Myrtle, and Mr. Martin and wondered if they were all in jail now. If they weren't, why hadn't she heard from them?

"That shows how much you know," said the woman angrily. "Woman has a great deal more political power now than she'd have if she got the vote. Right now, when a woman goes to her congressman or senator and asks him for something, he knows that she's completely disinterested; she has no political stake in what she's asking for."

"It seems to me that would only work if he doesn't have any political stake in what she's asking for either," Violet said.

"Young lady! Did you just contradict me?"

Violet thought about what she'd just said. "I guess so."

"You're a very badly brought-up young lady."

"No, I'm not," Violet contradicted again. "I'm a very well-brought-up young lady, but I'm getting over it."

She started to lift her bowl to her mouth to drink the last melted bit of pineapple ice but then decided she'd better not lose all her manners at once. She set the bowl down on a table.

"You know, when you think about it," Miss

Escuadrille was saying loudly nearby, "here it is 1920 already. I mean, doesn't it seem sort of, I don't know, crazy that women still haven't got the vote yet?"

"Annasette, hush. You don't know what you're saying," said Miss Pearson.

"Yes, I do," said Miss Escuadrille. "I may not be very smart, but I know when someone's trying to pull a fast one on me. We're women, so what are we doing fighting against women getting the vote?"

Miss Pearson opened her mouth to answer, then shut it as a page boy rushed into the room (followed by an Anti who was guarding him to make sure he arrived safely) and thrust a note into Miss Pearson's hand.

Everyone watched while Miss Pearson read the note. "The House is adjourned till tomorrow," she announced. "So it will go on another day."

There were murmurs all around. This was not good news for the Antis, Violet realized. They had been expecting a vote today, and an easy win.

18

August 18

CHLOE AND MYRTLE HAD STILL NOT SHOWN up. It was Wednesday, August 18. There had been meetings all night long at the Hermitage, both Suffs and Antis, and the sound of the elevator running up and down had combined with the stifling heat to keep Violet awake most of the night.

Violet could think of no way she could find out what had happened to Chloe and Myrtle and Mr. Martin. If she went to the police, would they even tell her? Would they arrest her and question her? Did those Palmer agents even have anything to do with the police?

What if they never came back? What would Violet do? Should she write to her parents for help? Would they even help her? Violet had to admit, though she didn't want to, that they probably would. They might come to Tennessee on a train, full of fury, to rescue her. Or they might call the police and tell them to arrest Violet and keep her in jail till they came. Was that what had happened to Hobie the Hobo?

Violet went down to the lobby, thinking about all this and about finding something to eat. But as soon as she stepped off the elevator, she was caught up in a tide of people surging toward Capitol Hill.

"You'd better hurry or you won't get a seat!" a woman called as they climbed. Violet didn't know her and couldn't tell whether the woman was a Suff or an Anti. There were hundreds of people climbing up the hill. Violet looked around for Chloe, but she didn't see her. What if she never saw Chloe again?

She spotted a yellow rose on the ground, and she picked it up and stuck it in her hat.

"If they're going to vote, it means the Antis are sure they're going to win," a woman near Violet said grimly.

Violet turned around and recognized Miss Kelley from the train. "Good morning, Miss Kelley," she said politely. "What do you mean?"

"Seth Walker controls when the vote happens," Miss Kelley said, panting as she climbed. "And the Antis own him. That's why the vote's been delayed so long; Walker's been waiting till he was sure."

Violet felt a sinking in her stomach. What Miss Kelley said made perfect sense. When she looked up to reply, Miss Kelley had vanished in the moving throng. There was still no sign of Chloe anywhere.

The crowd carried her into the dark, vaulted first floor of the capitol. They surged up the wide stone staircase with the bullet-gouged handrail. Violet looked around, hoping to see Chloe in the crowd, but elbows and shoulders closed in all around her, blocking her view.

In the light, high-ceilinged main floor of the capitol, everyone was pushing toward the House chamber. The doors were open, and people were pouring onto the House floor. Violet joined them. Soon she was one of hundreds of women crowded among the old mahogany desks in front of the high Speaker's dais. "Out, ladies, please! Out!" a harassed-looking man in a uniform was saying. "Spectators are forbidden on the floor. All up to the galleries, please."

He put his hand on Violet's shoulder. "Up to the gallery, please, miss." He gave her a little shove toward the door.

Violet went out. It was too crowded on the House floor, and she couldn't see what was going on very well from there anyway. She started toward the narrow stairs to the spectators' gallery. Then she noticed a folded paper on the stone floor.

It was an envelope. It was addressed *Harry T. Burn, Hermitage Hotel, Nashville, Tennessee.*

Violet held the envelope in her hand, uncertain what to do. It was a letter to Mr. Burn, and it might be important. But Mr. Burn was an Anti. He had danced with Chloe, and with Violet, and remained an Anti. Every list she'd seen had had him listed as an Anti.

The envelope was open. Violet looked around her. The high-ceilinged hall was full of people heading toward the galleries or toward the House floor or just milling about in confusion. The stone walls and ceiling rang with voices, and footsteps, and an occasional high-pitched, nervous laugh. You could feel the tension in the air, Violet thought. There was a sense that today really was the day, after yesterday's false alarm.

It was very wrong to read other people's mail, and Violet knew it. She thought about how angry she had been at Mother for reading her letters from Chloe. But this was different, she told herself. This letter had already been opened. She glanced around. Nobody was paying any attention to her. She slid the letter out of the envelope and unfolded it. This is very wrong, she thought, but she read it anyway.

Dear Son:

Hurrah and vote for suffrage! Don't keep them in doubt! I noticed some of the speeches against. They were bitter. I have been watching to see how you stood but have not noticed anything yet. Don't forget to be a good boy and help Mrs. Catt put the "rat" in ratification!

Your Mother

Violet folded the letter hastily and stuffed it back in the envelope. The letter was from Mr. Burn's mother, who sounded less distant than her own mother. She couldn't imagine Mother starting a letter to her with "Dear Daughter." But then, she couldn't imagine Mother writing a letter to her at all. She wondered if Mr. Burn was in the habit of listening to his mother—a lot of people were. She'd better get this letter back to him. He might not even have read it yet—so many letters and telegrams had been stolen over the last few days. If he had gotten it, maybe he needed to read it again to remind him that millions of women needed his vote and that one of those women was his mother.

Violet knew that the Suffs had once considered Mr. Burn "persuadable." Maybe it wasn't too late. She wove through the crowd and worked her way back into the House chamber, darting by the sergeant at arms and wending her way through the crowds of women and men wearing red and yellow roses. "Mr. Burn!" She looked among the dark mahogany desks. "Mr. Burn!"

There he was. Mr. Burn looked up from his desk, a guarded, nervous expression on his face. It was the expression all of the legislators had come to wear since Monday—they reminded Violet of Mr. Martin, being hunted by agents. "You dropped this, Mr. Burn." She held out the folded envelope.

Wordlessly he took the envelope, without looking at it, and stuck it in his jacket pocket. He didn't meet her eyes. Violet thought that was a bad sign, then thought maybe it was a good sign, since Mr. Burn thought Violet was an Anti.

The sergeant at arms was coming toward Violet—why

did he keep picking on her? There were at least a hundred women on the floor who weren't supposed to be there. Violet wove her way out of the chamber and into the great cross-shaped hallway again.

"Excuse me." A woman wearing a red rose tapped Violet on the shoulder. "Can you tell me where the ladies' lavatory is?"

Violet looked at the woman. She was tall and thin and in her forties. She was wearing a worn-out polka-dot dress and a broad-brimmed straw hat with tired-looking poppies on it. Everything about the woman looked tired. "I think it's at the top of the stairs."

"No, I looked," said the tired woman. "There's only a men's."

Violet looked. There was a huge oaken door with a sign over it that said *Gentlemen.*

"Well, maybe it's around the other side of the hall," said Violet, pointing.

"I looked there already," said the woman. "I don't think there is a ladies' lavatory." She looked close to panic.

"What do you expect?" said Violet, losing her patience. "Of course there's no ladies'. If you don't want women to vote and you don't want women to have any say in government, then why on earth do you expect to find a ladies' lavatory in the capitol?" She had raised her voice much more loudly than she should have; she knew she was being rude.

"What do you mean?" The tired-looking woman

looked shocked. "I never said anything about voting. I just want the lavatory. Goodness, you young people today have no manners at all." Tears started in her tired eyes, and Violet felt terrible for having been rude.

"I'm sorry," she said. "Maybe there's a lavatory over here." She gestured to the woman and went over to the other side of the huge, vaulted marble hall to a place where it looked like there might be a recess that could lead to a bathroom.

The woman followed her. "Why are there so many people here?" she said. "What's this all about, anyway?"

Violet stared at her. "We're here to fight for justice. For the right to vote. You're against it." She pointed to the woman's red rose, even though it was rude to point.

The tired woman touched her red rose gingerly. "Is that what this means? They just rounded all of us lady workers up at the mill and gave us red roses to wear and brought us up here in an omnibus."

Violet was too surprised to answer. She opened the door to what she'd thought was the ladies' room. It was a broom closet.

"Brooks, tell Turner that Governor Cox is on the phone," a man's voice snapped.

Violet looked around. They were next to an open office door. She peered in. Two men were standing over a telephone. The man with the receiver in his hand had a stern, thin face with a pointed nose. The other man, Brooks, was round and chubby. They glared at each other.

"Get Turner in here now," said the man with the pointed nose.

Brooks muttered something about "attempts to influence the vote."

"Of course it's an attempt to influence his vote! Now get him in here at once. We can't leave a presidential candidate hanging on the phone."

Brooks said, "Yes, Governor Roberts," and turned and walked out of the office.

The man with the pointed nose—Governor Roberts—looked up and saw Violet. He looked at the yellow rose on her hat. "He's not going to do it. Go get Turner for me, girl."

Violet paused on the threshold. She had never spoken to a governor before. She was almost sure you were supposed to curtsy when you did, but she had more important things on her mind. Chloe had said Governor Roberts was a Suff. He was the one who had called this special session in Tennessee. But some of the Suffs' strongest supporters had changed sides. People seemed to be changing sides every minute. Violet had no intention of helping out the wrong side.

"Are you still a Suff, Governor?" she asked.

"Of course I'm a Suff," the governor snapped. "And Governor Cox is a Suff. And he's going to be the next president of the United States, and he's right here on the phone—long distance, which is not cheap—and he wants to talk to Turner. Now run, kid!"

Violet turned and hurried back to the House chamber. She passed the tired-looking woman with the red rose, who was saying in great embarrassment to Brooks, ". . . a place where I could wash my hands?"

"The ladies' is down on the ground floor," Brooks said. "Here, let me show you where it is." He held out his arm to the tired-looking lady and guided her toward the stone staircase. It could not have been clearer that he wasn't going to look for Turner.

Violet ducked past the sergeant at arms and into the chamber. "Mr. Turner!" she called. She didn't know what he looked like. "Mr. Turner!" There was no answer. One thing all of the legislators had learned in the last few days was not to answer when they were called. With a flash of inspiration, Violet pulled off her hat and plucked the yellow rose from it. She stuck it inside her hat and clapped the hat back on her head. Then she grabbed a page boy. "Where's Mr. Turner?"

The page boy nodded toward a man who was studiously looking away from her. Violet went up to his desk. "Mr. Turner, there's an urgent phone message for you. Please come at once."

The man looked up at her sourly. He had heard a lot about urgent phone messages in the last few days.

"There really is," said Violet. "I'm not lying. It's from . . ." She took a deep breath, not sure if this was a mistake or not. "It's from Governor Cox. The presidential candidate."

Mr. Turner looked even more sour. "I know who Governor Cox is, miss." He got tiredly to his feet. Violet led him out of the House chamber (the sergeant at arms scowled and said, "Don't come back in here again, missy") and across the great hall to the office where the phone call was waiting.

Mr. Turner reached for the telephone, glaring at Violet at the same time. "All right, I'm here, miss. Now scram. Good morning, Governor."

Governor Roberts smiled at Violet. "Thanks, kid. Now run along."

Violet went back out into the hall. The crush of people moving up the narrow staircases to the spectators' gallery had slowed to a trickle. Violet went up the stone stairs to the gallery. It was swelteringly hot. From the balcony at the top of the stairs, she looked down at the cross-shaped hall. Still no Chloe.

Violet looked around the crowded gallery for a seat. There were none left. People were crammed into the aisles. There were deep windowsills, two feet deep and at least six feet wide, near the floor, and people were standing on them.

Violet wormed her way through the crowd to the brass rail at the front of the gallery. She stood behind the rail, with people pressing close all around her. She looked down at the House floor below. She hadn't had a good view of it when she was down there. The whole chamber was hung with yellow—yellow bunting, yellow flowers.

There was even a yellow sunflower wound around an eagle on the wall. Chloe wasn't down there either.

"There are too many red roses," a woman standing next to Violet murmured.

Violet looked up and saw Miss Dexter, the lady she'd ridden with on the train from Washington. "There's an awful lot of yellow," she said.

"Up here there is," said Miss Dexter. "But there are too many red roses down there."

Violet looked down at the floor again. Miss Dexter was right. More legislators were making their way into the chamber from the committee rooms alongside. Some wore yellow roses, but far too many wore red roses. Violet saw Credwell, the Suff legislator she had retrieved in the Hope Chest the day before. He was a Suff no longer. He was wearing a red rose.

"Did you notice Harry T. Burn has a red rose?" someone near Violet said. "Cross Burn off."

Miss Dexter winced. "We worked so hard on Burn," she said to Violet.

A ripple of excitement spread through the galleries as a man with a yellow rose made his way onto the floor. "Griffin!" Miss Dexter said. "Griffin made it back from California. Thank God."

A very pale, unhealthy-looking man limped out onto the floor, leaning on the shoulder of an aide. He wore a yellow rose on his lapel. Cheers broke out in the gallery.

"Dowlen!" Miss Dexter cried, cheering with the rest. "Dowlen! He's alive."

Seth Walker pounded his gavel. "Order! The House is in session. All non-members must leave the floor."

"Turncoat," Miss Dexter hissed, glaring at Walker. "Traitor. Benedict Arnold." A woman wearing a red rose turned around and scowled at Violet, apparently under the impression that she was the one who had spoken.

"Non-members, leave the floor!" Seth Walker commanded again.

There were plenty of non-members on the floor, men and women, pleading and cajoling with the representatives, trying to change their votes. Officials came around taking people by the arms and leading them off the floor over to the sidelines.

"We haven't got it," Miss Dexter murmured. "We haven't got it."

Other people around Violet were whispering the same thing. Violet felt her stomach do an anguished flip-flop. How was it possible? How could everything they'd worked so hard for fail?

"What do you mean, we haven't got it?" she demanded.

"We have forty-seven votes," said Miss Dexter. "Out of ninety-nine. Ninety-six members are present. And the Antis have forty-nine votes."

"That's impossible!" Violet said.

"Shh!" several people hissed.

"Count the roses for yourself," Miss Dexter snapped.

A young woman in a wide-brimmed hat turned around. Violet recognized Miss Anita Pollitzer. "Here's the list, Violet. See for yourself."

Violet took the paper Miss Pollitzer handed her. Names and tally marks had been crossed out and written over.

"But some of these people were ours yesterday!" Violet said, remembering to speak quietly. Debate had started on the floor below now. "Like Blotz and Credwell!"

"They certainly were," said Miss Pollitzer. "But they aren't now."

"But it's not fair!" Violet managed with difficulty to keep her voice low. "They can't have just sold their votes like that."

"Of course they can," said a woman near Violet, who was wearing a yellow sash. "All you need to buy votes is a whole lot of money and a few fools who actually agree with you."

Violet shook her head, rejecting this cynical view. She handed the paper back to Miss Pollitzer.

Miss Dexter clutched Violet's shoulder hard. "He's called for a vote!"

"What?" said Violet.

The murmur went around the gallery. "He's called the question. Mr. Walker's called for a vote. That means he's sure. He knows."

Knows the Antis have enough votes to win, thought Violet.

"So this really is the end," Miss Dexter said. Violet heard tears in her voice.

"It's not the end," she said, more because she wanted to comfort Miss Dexter than because she believed it. "There's Vermont."

"We can't get Vermont," someone said, and Violet whirled around to see Chloe.

"When did you get here?" Violet cried. "Is Mr. Martin—"

"Shh!" several people hissed at once.

"Yes," said Chloe. Violet thought she was answering the question about Mr. Martin, but what did "yes" mean?

"They're voting on a motion to table!" an Anti near Violet snapped. "What's that mean, 'table'?"

Miss Dexter frowned. "It means to not vote on ratification at all," she said. "To table the question—to put it aside. It's what North Carolina did. You blithering idiot," she added.

Several people around Miss Dexter gasped, and the Anti turned around and looked ready to slap Miss Dexter. "You take that back!"

"Oh, shut up and go back to your kitchen," Miss Dexter snarled. "Or wherever you think Woman's Sphere is."

Violet seized Miss Dexter by the arm and, with Chloe's help, led her away before a fight could start. The crowd squeezed aside to let them through. They found a space near the back. Violet and Chloe each kept a tight hold on one of Miss Dexter's arms.

"I'd like to rearrange her face for her," Miss Dexter said. "The idiotic traitor to her sex."

"Do it later," Violet suggested. "Look, we can see better from up here."

A cheer went up in the gallery. "Defeated!" someone cried.

"What happened?" Miss Dexter demanded.

A man near them turned around, beaming. "Looks like Mr. Turner's changed sides. He voted against the motion to table and it tied."

"Tied?" said Violet, confused.

"Forty-eight to forty-eight," the man said. "That kills a motion to table. Turner was an Anti, but he just voted against tabling, with the Suffs. He changed sides. Either that or he made a mistake."

He didn't make a mistake, Violet thought. He got a phone call.

"It's finished," Miss Dexter said. "Turner changing sides isn't enough. We have forty-eight, they have forty-eight." She stuffed her fingers into her mouth and began biting them.

"I don't believe it!" said the man in front of them. "That Seth Walker is making them vote to table again. Can he even do that? And now he's down there with his arm around Turner, talking in his ear."

Violet stood up on tiptoes and was just in time to see Turner shrug Seth Walker away from him, get to his feet, and vote against the motion to table again.

"Now he's calling the question!" someone said.

"He's calling the question." Everyone was murmuring and whispering it to each other. "This is it. Seth Walker's calling the question."

Violet desperately wanted to ask Chloe what had happened to Myrtle and Mr. Martin, but now wasn't the time. She and Chloe were on opposite sides of Miss Dexter, and a hush fell over the chamber and galleries that seemed to forbid even a whisper. Violet was still clutching Miss Dexter's arm, and Miss Dexter clutched hers now too. Violet didn't even especially like Miss Dexter—she couldn't forget about that business with Myrtle on the train—but right now they were clinging to each other as if their lives depended on it.

This was the vote that mattered.

"Anderson."

"Aye!"

"He was ours from the start," Miss Dexter murmured. "And he never wavered. Bless him."

"Bell."

"Aye."

"Bond."

"They bought him," Miss Dexter said through the fingers in her mouth. "Bought him like a . . . like a . . ."

"Pig in a poke," Violet suggested. She was far too

nervous to care whether it sounded right—or was even true.

"Forty-eight to forty-eight," Miss Dexter said again. "We have forty-eight, and they—"

"Shh!" the man in front of them hissed.

"Burn."

"Aye."

"Canale."

"What?" said Miss Dexter. She dropped Violet's arm in surprise. A murmur was sweeping through the gallery. "Burn? Harry T. Burn voted for ratification? But Burn is theirs. Burn is an Anti."

"He's ours now," the man in front of them barked. "Burn is ours! Burn changed his mind. If we can just keep Turner . . ." Violet nodded silently. Her voice wouldn't work. The clerk called off the men's names and they voted—aye, nay. There were no more surprises. . . . But would Turner vote aye?

"God, let us keep Turner," Miss Dexter breathed.

"Turner," the clerk called.

Silence fell for a moment that seemed to last much longer than it did. For some reason, Violet could hear Mrs. Catt's voice in her head, saying, *Seventy-two years, do you hear me? Seventy-two years!*

"AYE!"

"YES!" Miss Dexter fairly leapt into the air. Violet didn't realize until she felt her own feet hit the floor that she had done the same. All around them the air was full of hats and yellow roses being flung triumphantly upward. The women around Violet were screaming, crying, laughing, and dancing. The man in front of her turned around, seized Violet's and Chloe's hands, and began to dance an Irish jig.

Violet freed herself from the dance and climbed onto the wide windowsill. Down on the floor of the chamber, the legislators were dancing and cheering—at least, some of them were. Among the red rose wearers, only Turner and Burn were dancing. You had to say this for them, when they changed sides, they did it with enthusiasm. From above, showers of yellow rose petals fell on the legislators as people in the gallery made confetti out of their boutonnieres. The women who had been pushed to the sides of the chamber had come surging out and were leaping, singing, tap dancing. Violet saw a woman run up to Mr. Hanover, throw her arms around him, and kiss him on the cheek. Violet laughed delightedly. Everything seemed funny and wonderful.

Yes, she thought, yes, it was something to be here on this day.

It was sometime long after that, after the whole crowd had gone dancing and yelling down the stairs and out onto Capitol Hill together, that Violet remembered to ask Chloe, "What about Mr. Martin?"

"Shh. He's not Mr. Martin anymore. We've changed his name to Hanover, in honor of our friend from Memphis."

"But you got him out? On bail?"

"Not exactly," said Chloe. "But we did get him out. He and Myrtle . . . Oh, my goodness. No."

Chloe had her hand to her mouth and was staring up at the capitol building.

There was a man standing on the narrow stone ledge that surrounded the capitol, three stories above the pavement. His back and hands were pressed against the wall of the building.

"I hope he isn't going to jump!" said Chloe.

Violet noticed blond hair and a red rose. "I think it's Mr. Burn," she said. "How did he get out there?"

"Out the window, I suppose. Oh no, he's trying to walk along the ledge."

They watched helplessly as Mr. Burn edged his way along the narrow ledge. He looked very high up.

"Why doesn't he get down and crawl?" Violet asked.

"The ledge probably isn't wide enough," said Chloe. "Poor man, he must be running for his life. From the Antis."

They watched in anguish as Mr. Burn worked his way gingerly along the ledge in the hot sunlight. Nobody else seemed to have noticed him. Violet was wondering whether they should call for help, and if so, what kind of help. Then a window creaked open and a woman leaned out. Violet and Chloe watched as she spoke to Mr. Burn, then helped him inside.

"That's the library," said Chloe. "That's got him clear of the House chamber, anyway."

They started down Capitol Hill. "Myrtle and I got Theo out yesterday evening," said Chloe. "I'm sorry I didn't come tell you last night—but I didn't want to blow your cover."

"I blew my own cover," said Violet, and explained how.

"Good for you!" said Chloe. "Anyway, I've been up all night with Mrs. Catt and some other women, making phone calls to the two presidential candidates, Mr. Cox and Mr. Harding, and also to the White House to get them to call the Tennessee Anti legislators in their parties."

"You called the White House?" said Violet, impressed.

"No, Mrs. Catt did that. She and Woodrow Wilson have known each other for years. The president actually wired Seth Walker and asked him to change his mind—again—but Seth Walker said he couldn't go against his 'honest convictions.' Hmph. Even though they're not the same honest convictions he had a week ago."

In spite of having been up all night, Chloe was much more cheerful and less tired than she had been all week. Violet knew just how she felt. The world was a brighter and more hopeful place than it had been an hour ago.

"I think those phone calls helped," said Violet as they wandered through the capitol gardens toward the street. "They got Turner to change his vote."

"And that was all it took, Turner and Burn." Chloe shook her head, smiling. "To give twenty-seven million American women the vote. Isn't democracy amazing?"

"How did you get Mr. Mart—"

"Hanover," Chloe corrected.

"Mr. Hanover out?" This was confusing. "Did you, um, bail him out?" Violet wasn't sure how you got people out of jail, but she knew bail was involved somehow.

"Not exactly," said Chloe. "He and Myrtle are both at the municipal autocamp now. Come on. We'll take a streetcar."

"Why, where's the Hope Chest?" said Violet.

"I sold it," said Chloe, smiling.

"Sold it?" Violet couldn't imagine Chloe selling the Hope Chest. "Sold the Hope Chest? But you said the Hope Chest was your freedom!"

"But I was wrong," said Chloe, waving to a streetcar that was jangling toward them. "Freedom is freedom. The Hope Chest is just a car."

The streetcar stopped and they climbed on. Chloe dropped two nickels in the fare box.

"What did you sell it for?" Violet asked.

"For getting Theo out of jail," said Chloe. "The Hope Chest belongs to a graduate student at Fisk University now."

She looked happy about it.

19

Freedom

THEY TOOK THE STREETCAR OUT TO THE autocamp. The seats were all full and they had to stand. They didn't care. It seemed like nothing in the world could ever make them unhappy again.

The city had built the campground to accommodate the new sport of autocamping, which had become so popular these last few years. Motorists could pitch their tents in the camps for free and stay as long as they wanted. Everyone was traveling all over America—at least, everyone who could afford an automobile and some gasoline—and people said it was just like the old covered-wagon days, only faster. But not much faster, because the roads were so bad.

Chloe and Violet walked to a tent at the back that had been turned around so that its door faced away from the rest of the campground—to keep Mr. Martin better hidden, Violet guessed. But Mr. Martin was kneeling on the ground outside the tent, tending a fire. Myrtle stood beside him, clutching his shoulder possessively.

"There you are!" He jumped up and hugged Chloe, then reddened and stepped back. "I heard already. We won!"

"Theo, what have you done to your face?" Chloe demanded.

Violet thought his face looked rather bruised and battered, and he had a black eye. He had also been given a terrible haircut, it looked like with a pocketknife. But Mr. Martin touched his scar. "I'm not wearing that stuff."

"You washed it off!" Chloe accused. "Theo, you have to wear it. And stop washing it off. I paid fifty cents for the bottle." Chloe ducked into the tent and emerged a minute later holding a small glass bottle.

"I am not wearing Lady Janis Liquid Face Powder," Mr. Martin said firmly.

"You have to wear it," said Myrtle. "Miss Chloe sold her car to get you out of jail. So paint your scar and stay out of jail." She took the bottle from Chloe and handed it to Mr. Martin.

"You sold your car?" said Mr. Martin. Chloe nodded. "You shouldn't have done that."

"To get you out of twenty years in Fort Leavenworth? Sure, I should have."

Mr. Martin silently sat down on a log and let Chloe

dab Lady Janis Liquid Face Powder over his scar, his bruises, and his black eye. Myrtle and Violet watched with interest. The stuff was a little bit lighter than Mr. Martin's face but darker than the scar. Once Chloe put on several coats, you couldn't see the scar if you looked at him from a distance. Or you probably wouldn't if you didn't already know the scar was there, Violet thought. And on a darker day, maybe.

"Now we'll celebrate!" Mr. Martin said. "You ladies are about to taste the finest of Hungarian dishes: *rakott krumpli* and *zigeunerspeck*. Nothing else is good enough to celebrate the Nineteenth Amendment to the U.S. Constitution. At least, nothing that is legal in these abstemious times."

He reached into the tent and brought out a paper sack, from which he began pulling out potatoes, onions, eggs, a cut of bacon, and a paper twist of spices.

"Theo, you went grocery shopping?" Chloe said in dismay. "Anyone could have seen you."

"I only went to the camp store," said Mr. Martin with a shrug. He pulled out his pocketknife, which Myrtle had returned to him, and began peeling potatoes.

"You're hopeless," said Chloe, sitting down beside him and taking a knife from her handbag. "We have to get you out of the country quickly."

Although it was still sunny, a shadow seemed to have fallen over the campsite. They all drew closer to the fire as if for warmth, although it was a hot day. There was silence for a moment.

"I was thinking about Argentina," said Mr. Martin dismally, slicing into a potato. "They say it's very nice there."

"Do you speak Spanish?" Violet asked.

"No," said Theo. He set a naked potato on the toe of his boot and sliced it in half. "I've been meaning to learn."

"What about Alaska?" said Chloe.

Mr. Martin looked at her in surprise. "Why would I go to Alaska?"

"Because Alaska gave women the vote as its very first territorial act," said Chloe. "And because it is a territory, not a state, and they hardly have any laws there. And it's about five thousand miles away from Attorney General Palmer and his friend J. Edgar Hoover and their agents. And there are plenty of people there who have found it convenient to change their names."

"You seem to know a lot about Alaska," said Mr. Martin with a depressed-looking smile.

"She's wanted to go there all her life," Violet put in. She remembered the picture Chloe had drawn for her of an Eskimo driving a dogsled.

Mr. Martin picked up another potato and studied it thoughtfully. He looked at Chloe quickly and then back at the potato. "Do you want to go there, you know, I mean . . ." He stopped, at a loss for words, and stared at the potato.

"Do you want to go there with him, Miss Chloe?" Myrtle finished firmly. "Say yes."

"Excuse me," said Violet, jumping up. "I have to use the . . ." She stumbled blindly away from the campsite. She didn't have to use anything. She wandered between an autotent set up against the side of a Pan touring car and a red-and-white-striped tent that smelled strongly of mildew. She accidentally walked into the midst of a family sitting on the ground eating liverwurst sandwiches and pickles.

She knew it was dumb of her, but she'd just assumed Chloe would be going back to New York. She had gone on thinking that Chloe would let Violet live with her, even though Chloe had changed the subject every time she'd brought it up. She hadn't thought that Chloe—independent Chloe, who had spent her hope chest money on a car and called it her freedom—would ever get married. Well, lots of people said they never wanted to get married and then they went and got married just the same.

But they didn't go to Alaska when they did it.

Violet wandered over to the bathroom. It had real toilets and running water. She wandered on and found a kitchen house, with real stoves in it. All this for free, Violet thought. They shouldn't have wasted their money in the hotel. But she supposed it had been the National Woman's Party's money.

Chloe, Violet realized, had just come to the end of a long battle. Violet had cared about women winning the vote for the last week or so—ever since she met the woman waiting for her son's coffin in Chattanooga. And these last few days it had meant a great deal to her. But she hadn't fought for it like Chloe had. That Chloe would want to move on to something else now was normal, she supposed. That Mr. Martin should be the something else she wanted to move on to was . . . well, probably also normal. Only to be expected, really.

Mother and Father would be absolutely furious. Violet smiled. That was some consolation. *Furious* wasn't even the word for it. They had wanted Chloe to marry a Mr. R., not a one-eyed, seven-fingered Bolshevik who was on the run from the law and kept changing his name.

By the time she got back to the campsite, Chloe and Mr. Martin were standing side by side with their arms around each other, and Chloe's spare arm was around Myrtle.

"I've always wanted to go to Alaska too," Myrtle was saying.

Violet decided to ignore all this. "There's a kitchen over there, with stoves," she said. "You don't need to use the campfire."

"But we have to have a campfire or we're not really camping!" Mr. Martin said enthusiastically. He disentangled himself from Chloe long enough to flip the bacon in the frying pan resting in the flames. "In Alaska we'll cook like this all the time! No stoves in Alaska."

"It's very cold there," Violet reminded him. "Most of the year it's all snow and ice."

"And dogsleds!" Chloe said. "And mountains!" She patted Myrtle on the head. "We'll have to wrap Myrtle up in a caribou parka to keep her warm."

Violet burned with jealousy.

She knew that she had a home to go back to—she didn't want to go back to it, but she could—and Myrtle didn't. She knew that Mr. Martin had to leave the country or go to jail. But it wasn't fair. She had brought all of them together, found Chloe for Mr. Martin. And for Myrtle. And Myrtle and Mr. Martin for Chloe. That the three of them should all go off to Alaska and leave her was completely unfair.

"I want to go to Alaska too," Violet said.

The three of them looked at her. Their faces were all sad, as if they all knew she wasn't going to Alaska.

"Let's eat," said Mr. Martin.

They ate off tin plates, which, like the tent, Chloe had because she'd done a lot of autocamping during her travels from state to state over the last year. Violet had to admit that the stuff Mr. Martin had cooked was good, whatever it was called. It certainly didn't look like any of the things he'd put into it.

"How did you two meet each other?" Myrtle asked.

Chloe looked at Mr. Martin adoringly. "He hit me on the head with a shovel," she said.

"I did not!" Mr. Martin dropped his fork and tried to look annoyed but ruined it by looking adoring at the same time. "You walked into me. I was just carrying a shovel at the time."

"Why were you carrying a shovel?" Myrtle asked.

Mr. Martin and Chloe both looked suddenly solemn.

"I know," said Violet. "It was during the Influenza. She was coming home from seeing influenza patients, and he was coming home from . . . from digging graves for them."

Suddenly Violet felt that she couldn't wait to be grown up and allowed to work, all day and into the night if she wanted, on something that mattered. Not taking care of sick people, necessarily, and definitely not digging graves, but some important work that needed doing. She wanted to feel again the way she'd felt this last week in Nashville: that what she was doing was going to make a difference to somebody. The way she'd felt when her class knitted blankets for French orphans.

She thought about what Chloe had said, that college armed you to fight the great battles. She thought she knew what battle she needed to be armed for. She wanted to fight against the laws that put Myrtle in a separate train car and kept her out of hotels and away from drugstore lunch counters. Remembering the flat expressions on the faces of the desk clerks and the conductor, she realized that was a battle that could last a lifetime.

And she knew, just as well as Chloe and Myrtle and Mr. Martin knew, that she wasn't going to Alaska.

A week later Violet sat alone on a fence in front of the autocamp. She was waiting for some of the National Woman's Party ladies from New York, who had driven a big Packard motorcar to Tennessee. Violet was going to ride back with them, autocamping the whole way. Autocamping was America's most popular new sport, but Mother and Father had always said that it was unsuitable for ladies and that one met entirely the Wrong Sort of People while autocamping. Violet hoped this was true. She expected she might like the Wrong Sort of People just fine. It would be an exciting trip, and Violet would be in charge of taking notes on the condition of the roads, which the ladies could then report to their automobile club and to the newspapers back home. The only bad thing about the trip was that there was a serious risk Violet might get back to Susquehanna in time to start school.

Mr. Martin/Hanover/Arpadfi and Chloe had gotten married under the name of Hanover, which Violet was a little worried about because she wasn't sure it counted. They had gotten a justice of the peace in another county to marry them, a county where Mr. Martin had not been in jail and wouldn't be recognized. Getting married seemed to be the one occasion in Tennessee when it was all right to have white and colored people in a room at the same time, and nobody tried to chase Myrtle out.

It had been a very brief ceremony, because when the judge asked Chloe if she promised to love, honor, and obey Mr. Martin, Chloe had said, "Obey him? What is that doing in there? I certainly don't."

"Yes, really, that's a bit archaic," Mr. Martin had said. "She's not my dog, you know. Don't you have a

more modern marriage ceremony in there that you could do?" He reached politely for the book the judge was holding.

"Do you two want to get married or not?" the judge demanded.

"Yes, of course," said Chloe, and Mr. Martin said, "That's what we're here for."

"Fine. I now pronounce you man and wife," said the judge, slamming his book shut.

"Why not woman and husband?" said Chloe.

"I was already a man when I came in here," said Mr. Martin.

But the judge was through with them.

The Antis had tried for several days to get the Tennessee House to overturn their ratification of the Nineteenth Amendment, but instead the House voted and passed the amendment again. Then Governor Roberts signed the ratification and sent it by express to Secretary of State Colby in Washington, while the Antis kept sputtering and objecting and filing lawsuits.

Meanwhile, Chloe and Mr. Martin—Hanover—found someone who could give them and Myrtle a ride to Chicago. From there they would figure out a way to get to Seattle with Myrtle. Seattle was where ships for Alaska sailed from.

"But isn't that jumping bail?" Violet asked "Doesn't Mr. Mart—Hanover have a court date or something?"

"Please call me Theo," said Mr.—well, all right,

Theo, Violet decided. "According to what my wife tells me, I'm not out on bail."

"He's not?" said Violet to Chloe.

"Uh-uh," said Chloe happily. "Myrtle introduced me to a gentleman named Mr. Ezekiel, who she said knew a lot about bribes. Well, not a gentleman, exactly, but a Suff legislator. He knew exactly how to go about it. But I had to sell the Hope Chest to pay the bribe, which means I did use the money Granny Mayhew left me to get married after all," Chloe said with a sigh. "Just like Granny meant me to."

"I doubt your granny meant for you to spend it on a bribe to get your fella out of jail," said Theo comfortingly.

Chloe brightened. "That's true. And I did make a lot of miles in the Hope Chest."

"You have an education to get, Violet," Chloe had told her before they'd left for Chicago. "You need high school—but don't take the domestic science program. Take sciences or academic, whichever you prefer. And then college. Remember what I said. College arms you to fight the great battles."

"And how am I supposed to get Father and Mother to agree to all that?" Violet said.

"Insist," said Chloe. "It won't cost them anything. There's your hope chest money."

Two weeks ago Violet would have replied that it was no good *insisting* with Father, who seldom even spoke to

her, or with Mother, who had no opinions except Father's. She would have said that the hope chest money might be hers in theory, but in reality it was tied up to a future she dreaded.

But now she knew what it was like to stand your ground. She knew what it was like to keep on when things seemed hopeless. And she knew that with patience and hard work, a radical, ridiculed idea—like women voting—could become as acceptable and ordinary as oatmeal.

Historical Notes

Real People

ALTHOUGH VIOLET, MYRTLE, CHLOE, AND MR. Martin are fictional, most of the characters who appear in *The Hope Chest* are real, including Alice Paul, Lucy Burns, Harry T. Burn, Joe Hanover, Hobie the Hobo, and Carrie Chapman Catt. The arguments used for and against women voting are all real too. In 1920 many Americans believed they were living at the dawn of a golden age, when war, alcohol, and poverty were about to vanish from the earth. Others believed that the United States was on the verge of a communist revolution.

A few characters, including Mr. Ezekiel, Mr. Blotz, and Mr. Credwell, are made-up people whose stories really happened. History has been too polite to record the real people's names. You can read about them, and much more about the final showdown in Nashville, in *The Perfect 36: Tennessee Delivers Woman Suffrage,* by Carol Lynn Yellin and Janann Sherman.

Miss Dexter is invented, but her attitude is not. Some suffragists were racists. Some of them would have liked to get the vote only for white women, but most realized that this was unreasonable.

Woman Suffrage—Lost and Gained

AMERICAN WOMEN REGAINED THE RIGHT TO VOTE in 1920, 113 years after they lost it. Women could and did vote in several states in the early years of our nation. The last state to revoke the vote for women was New Jersey, in 1807.

Forty-one years later, in 1848, women began fighting to regain the vote at the Women's Rights Convention in Seneca Falls, New York. Among the speakers at the convention were three antislavery leaders: Elizabeth Cady Stanton, Lucretia Mott, and Frederick Douglass. During these early years, the woman suffrage movement and the abolitionist movement worked closely together. Freeing both

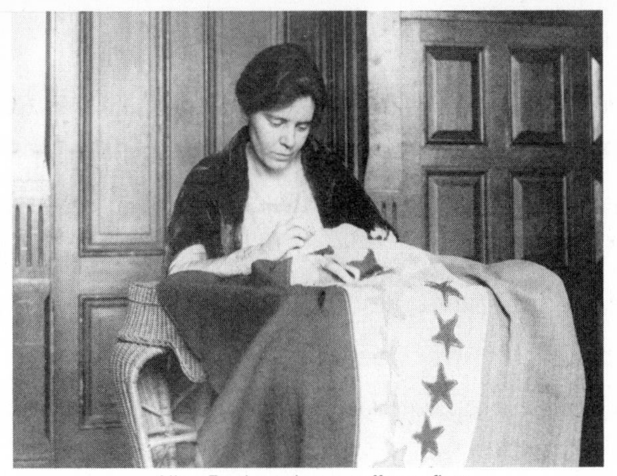
Alice Paul sewing a suffrage flag

women and African Americans seemed to be two parts of the same goal.

After the Civil War, the states ratified the Thirteenth, Fourteenth, and Fifteenth amendments to the Constitution, ending slavery and giving African American men full citizenship and the right to vote. Some suffragists reacted with resentment. The Fourteenth Amendment put the word *male* into the U.S. Constitution for the first time—before that, it had been the individual states, not the federal government, that denied women the right to vote.

Suffragist leader Susan B. Anthony wrote the amendment that eventually became the Nineteenth Amendment. It was first introduced into Congress in 1878 but was voted down. At the time of Anthony's death in 1906, only a handful of Western states and territories allowed women to vote.

Starting in the West and spreading to the Northeast, from Wyoming in 1869 to New York in 1917, the men in various states gradually agreed to let their sisters vote. No Southern state gave women full voting rights. The state-by-state fight for woman suffrage seemed slow and wasteful to Alice Paul, a Quaker suffragist from Pennsylvania. In 1916 Paul founded the National Woman's Party, with the goal of getting Congress and the states to pass the Susan B. Anthony Amendment. In this way, states where women were already voting could help bring the vote to states that might otherwise never let women vote.

Congress passed the Susan B. Anthony Amendment in 1919. When it became part of the Constitution in 1920, only one woman who had attended the 1848 Women's Rights Convention in Seneca Falls was still alive—Charlotte Woodward Pierce.

People believed that woman suffrage would bring about great changes, such as an end to war, child labor, alcoholism, and corruption. It was expected that women would all vote the same way. They didn't. Some people say that women ended up voting "whichever way their husbands did," but with the secret ballot, that's impossible to know.

As soon as the Nineteenth Amendment was ratified, Alice Paul began working on an equal rights

Miss Maude Younger, legislative secretary of the National Woman's Party, working on her Ford with her dog, Sandy

amendment. She continued working on this until her death in 1977. Thirty-five states ratified it. It never became law.

Despite his good deed on the morning of August 18, Governor Cox lost to Warren G. Harding in the 1920 election. (By the summer of 1920, both Harding and Cox were Suffs, just in case.) Harding's administration was plagued by scandal, but he did pardon the "Bolsheviks" who were still in prison for having spoken out against the War.

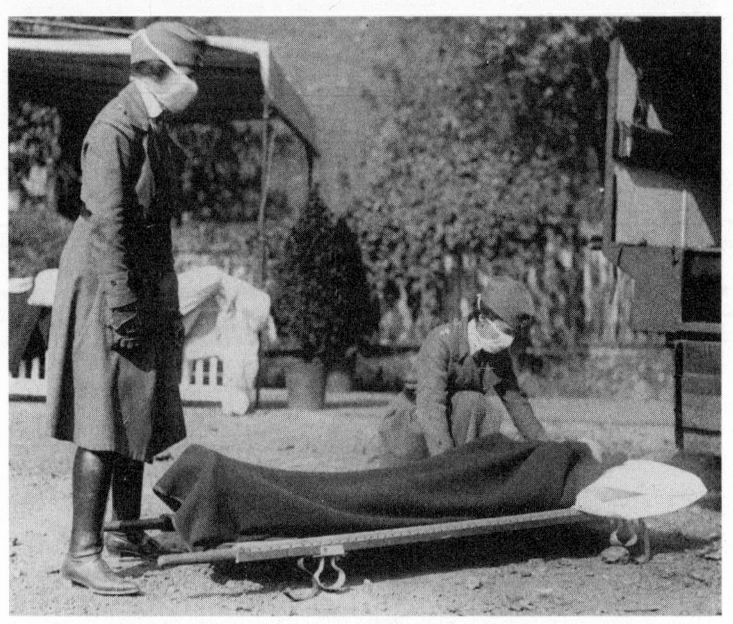

Demonstration at the Red Cross Emergency Ambulance Station in Washington, D.C., during the influenza pandemic of 1918

The Influenza

THE GLOBAL INFLUENZA PANDEMIC WAS A FORM OF bird flu. It started out as a fairly mild disease in the U.S. in the spring of 1918. By autumn it had traveled through Europe and Asia and back to the U.S., and had mutated into a deadly disease which killed an estimated 20 to 50 million people worldwide. At the time, it was called the Spanish Influenza because Spain, a neutral country in World War I, reported a high death toll. The warring countries also had high death tolls but didn't report them because they didn't want to reveal any weakness to their enemies.

World War I

WORLD WAR I BEGAN IN 1914 WHEN THE GERMAN army overran Belgium and invaded France. It officially ended on November 11, 1918, although sporadic fighting continued for many years. It was ultimately one of the root causes of World War II in 1939.

The United States entered the War in 1917 and began sending large numbers of drafted and volunteer American soldiers (many carrying influenza) overseas in 1918. The arrival of the strong American reinforcements, combined with a revolution in Germany, led to a German surrender.

Poster urging women to help the war effort, 1918

Jim Crow Laws

THE THIRTEENTH, FOURTEENTH, AND FIFTEENTH amendments to the U.S. Constitution ended slavery and made African Americans full citizens, but some states passed laws to keep blacks out of sight and out of public life. Public facilities were segregated throughout the South, and some states required "literacy tests" for voting. The tests were so complicated that nobody, black or white, could pass them, so the laws also contained a "grandfather clause." The clause stated that you did not have to pass the test if your grandfather voted—that is, if you had a white grandfather. These laws were repealed in the 1960s as a result of the civil rights movement.

Civil rights march on Washington, D.C., 1963

Voting in America: A Time Line

EIGHTEENTH CENTURY: MOST OF THE COLONIES have some form of elected government. Only property owners can vote. In some colonies voting is restricted based on race, sex, and religion, but the most important qualification is wealth.

1776: The Declaration of Independence, written by slave owner Thomas Jefferson, states that "all men are created equal."

1777: Women lose the right to vote in New York.

1780: Women lose the right to vote in Massachusetts.

1784: Women lose the right to vote in New Hampshire.

1787: The U.S. Constitution is ratified. It gives each state the right to determine the qualifications for voting. Most states restrict voting to male property holders over age twenty-one; some states bar free African Americans from voting.

1801: Residents of Washington, D.C., lose the right to vote.

1807: Women lose the right to vote in New Jersey, the last state to allow women to vote.

1848: The Women's Rights Convention takes place in Seneca Falls, New York.

1856: North Carolina gets rid of the wealth requirement for voting—the last state to do so.

1867: The Fourteenth Amendment makes African Americans citizens but defines voters as "male."

1870: The Fifteenth Amendment gives African American males the right to vote.

1878: Congress rejects the Susan B. Anthony Amendment.

1880s: A series of laws known as the Chinese Exclusion Act deny Chinese Americans citizenship.

1887: The Dawes General Allotment Act states that Native Americans can vote only if they resign from their tribes.

1898: U.S. Supreme Court rules that U.S.-born children of immigrants are citizens.

1920: The Nineteenth Amendment gives women the right to vote.

1924: The Indian Citizenship Act makes Native Americans citizens, with the right to vote.

1943: The Chinese Exclusion Act is repealed; Chinese Americans gain the right to vote.

1946: Filipinos gain the right to become U.S. citizens and to vote.

Three suffragists casting votes in New York City, 1917

1952: The McCarran-Walter Act gives first-generation Japanese Americans the right to become U.S. citizens and to vote.

1961: The Twenty-third Amendment gives residents of Washington, D.C., the right to vote in presidential elections only.

1964: The Twenty-fourth Amendment eliminates poll taxes, which had been used to restrict voting in the South.

1965: The Voting Rights Act eliminates so-called literacy tests, which had been used to keep African Americans from voting in some Southern states, and gives the federal government power to oversee voter registration and fair elections in some areas.

1971: The Twenty-sixth Amendment lowers the voting age from twenty-one to eighteen nationwide.

1973: The Home Rule Act gives residents of Washington, D.C., the right to elect a mayor and city council.

1974: The Supreme Court rules that states may deny felons the right to vote.

1978: Congress passes the D.C. Voting Rights Amendment, which would have given Washington, D.C., residents representation in Congress. Only sixteen states ratified it.

Acknowledgments

NASHVILLE, TENNESSEE, IS A REMARKABLE CITY IN many ways. One way is that if you walk around downtown with a notebook, total strangers will come up and offer to answer your questions. Consequently, I owe thanks to many Nashvilleans whose names I do not know.

In addition, I would like to thank the Nashville Room staff at the Nashville Public Library; Janann Sherman and the late Carol Lynn Yellin, authors of *The Perfect 36: Tennessee Delivers Woman Suffrage,* much of whose research I have used, with Dr. Sherman's permission; David Andrews, the concierge at the

Hermitage Hotel (which does not have the same owners as it did in 1920, and *certainly* not the same policies); Alison Oswald, Susan Strange, and Kay Peterson at the Archives Center, National Museum of American History, Smithsonian Institution, for instruction in the lost art of sending telegrams; Jennifer Spencer at the Sewall-Belmont House and Museum for information about Cameron House; Donna Melton, Rose A. Simon, Paul Odom, and the staff at Gramley Library, Salem College; Aaron, Jennifer, and Deborah Schwabach for reading and suggestions; and my editor, Lisa Findlay, whose idea this book was.

About the Author

KAREN SCHWABACH HAS BEEN VOTING SINCE 1984. She grew up in upstate New York and graduated from Antioch College and the State University of New York at Albany. She spent many years in Alaska, where she taught English as a Second Language in the remote Yup'ik (Inuit) village of Chefornak, on the Bering Sea coast. She currently lives in upstate New York. *The Hope Chest* is her second novel.